THE GOVERNESS

LOUISA PENHALE

BLACK SWAN
DIGITAL

First published in 2025
Concept created by Black Swan Digital. Developed by Annie Kenyon.

1

The mail coach laboured through the Cotswold hills, its wheels thick with mud from the Oxford road. Morning drizzle clung to the hedgerows, mist softening the lines of the fields and the land seemed to hold its breath, waiting for the intruders to pass.

Inside the carriage sat a solitary passenger. A young woman in dark travelling clothes, her gloved hands folded in her lap. A thin veil shaded her face, revealing enough to suggest refinement where weariness might have been expected. From time to time she leaned forward, watching the blur of grey through the window. Her reflection vanished into the fog as if the world had swallowed her.

The driver called to his horses, the sound harsh in the stillness and the woman flinched, whispering under her breath some scripture, half remembered. "Behold, I make all things new."

The name stitched into the small trunk at her feet read F.M. To the world, she was Miss Florence Marchwood. The trunk looked newly cleaned but second-hand, the brass latches worn smooth. No jewellery, no ornament, nothing to invite attention. Yet her stillness had control that didn't belong to modest means.

Her posture was too deliberate. Her expression, when unobserved, too intent as if she were listening for something far away.

The coach crested the final hill. Below lay the valley of Branleigh where green, faintly luminous fields folded toward the horizon like drapery. At the far edge, half-shrouded by oak and mist, stood a house: tall gables, thin smoke rising, pale honey stone catching what light the morning allowed.

The woman stirred. She leaned closer to the glass, breath clouding the pane. Her fingers rested against it, as if to test the image. “My new home,” she whispered. The words trembled between reverence and disbelief.

When the coach turned into the long drive, crows lifted from the lawn in a black ripple. Branleigh Park appeared in full grandeur, symmetrical, faintly oppressive in its precision. The steps were flanked by urns of dead geraniums, the upper windows closed tight as sealed eyes. The house seemed to watch without wishing to be seen. The door opened before the horses halted. The butler, grey-haired and stiff with habit, stepped beneath the portico. A footman followed, hurrying to open the carriage door.

Miss Marchwood descended with quiet composure. Rain had darkened her skirt, yet she moved without hesitation, gaze sweeping the façade as if committing it to memory.

“Miss Marchwood, I presume. Mr Carter,” he said, bowing. “You are expected.”

“Indeed, Mr Carter. I trust the household is well?”

“Well enough, miss.” His tone carried no warmth. “This way, if you please.”

The scent of beeswax and woodsmoke wrapped around her as she entered. The hall was vast, black-and-white marble underfoot, portraits of ancestors watching from dark varnish. A tall clock ticked steadily, its pendulum glinting like a blade. The servants hovered in corners, poking heads from doors to take a peek at the newcomer.

Florence paused. Something restless moved beneath her calm. Fear, or memory. To the servants, it would look only like a deep breath before composure returned.

"This way, miss. Her ladyship will see you after luncheon. You are to wait in the east parlour."

"Thank you," she said. Her voice was low, even, controlled.

Servants watched her pass and muttered. Too well-spoken for a one of them, too simply dressed for a lady. The cook whispered that she looked like a ghost come in out of the rain. The housemaid crossed herself.

Left alone in the east parlour, Florence went to the window. The mist was lifting. Gardens spread out below, the faint outline of a church beyond. A bell tolled slow and mournful. It drew a small smile from her.

"So," she murmured. "The Lord my shepherd has led me here."

Her fingers traced the glass. A sensation flickered as though she'd stood in such a room before, waiting unseen. A flash of heat, the weight of a locked door. She closed her eyes until the vision thinned to silence and the hiss of rain. When the butler returned, she was composed again. To him, merely a quiet woman of education and poise. Yet as she followed him upstairs, she glanced at a mirror on the landing and caught, for an instant, another face staring back who was younger, frightened, and gone before she blinked.

"Through here, miss."

Florence smoothed her gloves and stepped forward. She had arrived.

The drawing room stretched long and pale, the air faint with lavender and smoke, curtains softened the light to a dusty glow over portraits and marble. Near the fire stood Lady Georgina Spencer, elegant, brittle, her beauty refined and restrained. Her gown of grey silk hung in perfect order, a single pearl brooch at her collar. Her expression as Florence entered was thoughtful, assessing.

"Miss Marchwood," she said, extending a cool hand. "You have travelled far, I think?"

"Yes, my lady. The roads were heavy, but I am grateful to arrive safely."

The voice was calm, steady. Not eager to please, merely pleasant and factual. Georgina gestured to a chair.

"You will find Branleigh quiet. My children are gentle, although Hattie, the elder, has spirit. We value obedience, piety, and discretion here above all else."

Florence folded her hands. "Those are virtues I also hold dear, my lady."

Humble words, yet the undercurrent of certainty unsettled Georgina's composure.

"Tell me of your previous post," Georgina said.

"A clergyman's household near Cheltenham. One child. They went abroad for the father's health."

"You are not planning to be married?"

A pause. "No, my lady." The faintest smile. Controlled. Empty.

The door opened. A man's voice, easy and amused. "Ah, the new arrival."

Lord Charles Spencer entered, the warmth in his manner sounded frayed at the edges, false. Handsome in the careless way of privilege he had fair hair, grey eyes, and a voice where charm had worn thin. He offered his hand. "Welcome to Branleigh, Miss Marchwood. Forgive the gloom of the day."

"We have no control of the weather, your lordship. It is a fine house," she said. "It has the serenity of years."

He smiled. "Serenity, yes, that is my mother's doing.

Although she'll tell you the roses have never been the same since my father died."

Georgina's lips tightened. "Charles, Miss Marchwood has travelled far."

"Of course." His gaze lingered a moment too long. Florence lowered her eyes, colour rising briefly before she turned to the window.

A figure moved through the garden, a woman in grey, leaning on a cane. Even from here, her stature carried its own message.

"Lady Beatrice," said Georgina. "She walks when the weather allows."

"She must be strong," Florence said quietly.

"She is, and kind," Georgina added. "I hope you will please her."

"Kindness is nearest to God," Florence replied.

Georgina regarded her, unreadable. Then she rose. "You will dine in the nursery. The nurse, Annie Larkin, will show you the children."

"Your generosity humbles me," Florence said. "I hope to be worthy of it."

As she turned, Charles spoke. "Do you play the piano?"

"Indifferently, my lord."

"Then favour us sometime. My wife's music room has been silent too long."

Georgina's look was pure frost. He only smiled. "Silence breeds melancholy."

Florence met his gaze, steady. "And in silence, one hears all manner of things one ought not." The pause that followed hung heavy.

Dismissed, she followed Mr Carter down the hall. Portraits lined the corridor, their faces fading into shadow. At the end, one of a woman holding an infant. The light caught the child's pale face while the mother's was lost in darkness.

"The late Lady Spencer," the butler said. "Her ladyship's mother. Died young."

Florence studied the painting. "He looks so alone."

"It is a girl, miss, our Lady Georgina."

"Ah." A small smile. "Of course."

At the nursery door she paused. A woman's voice murmured beyond, low and rhythmic, the soft whimper of a child between words. Florence laid her palm against the panel, as if feeling the house breathe.

Her lips moved. "Hush now, little one. I've come back." She smoothed her skirt, lifted her hand, and knocked.

Inside, the nursery glowed with a fire that burned bright and steady. Toys were stacked neatly on shelves; a half-finished sampler rested on a chair. A young nurse looked up, red-haired, kind-faced, with exhaustion about the eyes. "You must be Miss Marchwood. The children are asleep."

Florence nodded, her gaze moving to the cradle near the hearth. Two small forms slept there, one stirring, one utterly still. She stepped closer. The sight of the infant's delicate hand curling in dream drew a flicker of emotion, too brief to name.

"I am grateful to you," Florence said softly. "You must have much to manage alone."

"Her ladyship keeps me busy, miss. They're good little souls, though." Annie hesitated. "You'll find them easy to love."

Florence smiled faintly. "I shall try."

When Annie turned away, Florence lingered. Her eyes fixed on the shadows in the corner, where the firelight failed to reach. A scent of damp wool and smoke hung in the air, familiar, almost comforting. She whispered again, so softly it might have been the room itself speaking.

"This house may be different, but my heart still remembers."

2

Morning arrived pale and thin, sunlight bleeding through the mist that pooled in Branleigh's hollows. From the village beyond the woods, church bells tolled, their sound drifting across wet meadows where sheep grazed and farmhands toiled. Inside the house, the day came to order with maids bearing breakfast trays for the nursery and the dowager's rooms, fires coaxed to life in library and drawing room, servants' boots ticking across stone.

Florence watched from her window. Below, Lord Charles mounted his bay and vanished into the whiteness with an ease she could not admire. She noted the hour by the mantel clock; exactly thirty minutes later the day's visitors filed through the door, the fishmonger with his basket wrapped against the damp, the post-boy shaking rain from his cap, a village woman with eggs cushioned in straw. The sequence pleased her. Branleigh moved like a well-tuned instrument. She would learn its tune, note by note, and then decide how to play it.

The nursery stood warm from the banked fire. Annie Larkin, the nurse, had the quick hands and tired eyes of a woman who rarely sat. Hattie chattered as Florence plaited her hair, listing all the names a person could give a pet snail.

"Pick one," Florence said.

"I can't," Hattie declared. "What if he dislikes it and slimes away?"

"The considerate solution," Florence said, "is to ask him."

Hattie considered the snail in its jam-jar kingdom and lowered her voice. "Would you like to be called Hector?"

The snail offered no opinion. Hattie beamed. "He blinked! He likes it."

Across the room, Theodore clumsily stacked wooden bricks with his chubby hands and Florence praised his attention to detail. He glanced up, uncertain whether she was teasing. She wasn't. He relaxed and the next line straightened. When lessons ended, a maid appeared with a summons. Lady Beatrice wished to receive the new governess for tea in the east parlour.

The dowager sat near the window, a shawl folded neatly across her knees, a thin volume lay open, face-down beside the tea service. Light caught the silver in her hair and turned her skin almost translucent; her eyes remained bright, steady.

"Miss Marchwood," she said, offering a small, cool hand. "You have already earned polite reports. How do you find my grandchildren?"

"They are a pleasure, my lady," Florence said, taking the opposite chair. "Miss Hattie has a busy mind. Master Theodore prefers a gentler pace. Between them they will assemble a small empire by the age of ten."

Beatrice's smile began in the eyes. "And the emperor?"

"Hector the snail," Florence said. "A benevolent monarch."

A soft laugh. "It is well you have humour. A governess needs patience and a strong spine, too. The post can be... particular."

"I know it," Florence said. "I will do what is required."

Beatrice studied her without hurry. "Forgive me. There is a

likeness I cannot place. For a moment, when you stood in the doorway…" She shook her head. "Memory plays tricks."

"I have lived many places," Florence said evenly. "There is always someone who looks like someone else."

"Perhaps." Beatrice poured the tea herself. Her hands trembled only slightly. "You are welcome, Miss Marchwood. Branleigh has suffered its share of stale air. New spirits do a house good."

Florence glanced to the window. The rose garden lay stripped to bone, each cane bright with frost. "You are kind, my lady."

A knock. Mr Carter entered with the post upon a salver. Beatrice sorted through with practised fingers.

"For her ladyship," she murmured, laying a thick envelope aside, "and household bills. And ah. A pamphlet from the Society for the Relief of Prisoners' Families. Charles says they never leave off."

"Perhaps they shouldn't," Florence said before she could tidy the thought away.

Beatrice's eyes warmed. "I think so too." She set the papers down and returned to the safer ground of children's health and the temper of the winter. Yet something in Florence's restraint, the press of feeling without the display perhaps, seemed to please her. When the tea was done she rose with effort, and Florence rose with her.

"You may come to me if you need anything," Beatrice said. "Do not waste days finding roundabout ways."

"I will remember," Florence said. She meant it.

After dinner, Georgina joined her mother-in-law in the same room. Charles unfolded his newspaper and pretended to read. The talk moved through weather, parish business, the new plough in the south field, and, as naturally as water finds a slope, to the nursery.

"She does well enough," Georgina said. "The children like her. But..." she paused, then shrugged as if discarding an unworthy thought. "She is rather striking and perhaps a distraction amongst the servants."

Beatrice's mouth tilted. "Beauty is not a failing."

"No," Georgina said, colouring. "Only that she carries herself with such self-possession one forgets her position."

Charles looked up, amused. "Pretty governesses improve a household's temper. This place can be funereal."

Beatrice sent him a look. Georgina let the remark pass. The fire settled, the hour grew late, the room thinned to the click of cooling embers.

In the corridor outside, unseen, Florence had stopped by the half-open door to retrieve a forgotten shawl. She heard the exchange entire. For a moment she stood very still, her hand pressed to the base of her throat where her pulse had jumped. Heat rose under her skin, not merely shame and not quite pride.

"Pretty," she said under her breath, trying the shape of it. The word floated between promise and warning. She slipped the shawl around her shoulders and walked back through the quiet house to the nursery where the children breathed in sync with the one another.

Annie looked up from her mending. "They're settled," she whispered.

Florence nodded and crossed to Theodore. In sleep his face lost its solemnity. She tucked his blanket, smoothed his hair, and waited until the taut line of his mouth loosened. Hattie slept curled toward the cradle she insisted on sharing with her brother, one hand tucked underneath her cheek, the other resting on the jam jar that housed Hector. Florence lifted the jar, moved it to the shelf, and only then noticed the faint burn-mark on the underside of the wooden lid. A tiny crescent, as if a coal had kissed it.

"Old damage," Annie said softly at her shoulder. "Before you ask. From another winter."

Florence closed her hand over the lid. "Another winter," she repeated, and set it down.

The house emptied toward sleep. Georgina, however, remained by the fire with her thoughts. Beatrice retired with her maid and Charles fell away to his own diversions in his study. Only the clock remained, persuading the night forward with its patient beat.

Outside, wind shouldered the windows. Rain feathered the panes. The sound drew Georgina back to Radcliffe Hall and the disciplined corridors of her father's house, the garden walks conducted at the correct time in all weathers. She remembered a governess whose patience had been steel wrapped in velvet, and the way praise had arrived only in the absence of fault. Her father had loved order. Obedience, in his view, was an art.

She had been twenty when Charles Spencer first filled the dining room with his light, bright talk. He had looked at her as if she were worth looking at. The marriage was arranged almost before she had formed a wish. She had entered it with that useful, well-bred hope that affection follows duty. At first he had tried. He showed her every polished room, walked her through fields he described as if they were his own design. But attention curdled into carelessness, then into a need for admiration she could not supply. When she failed to mirror back his best self, he went elsewhere for the reflection. She told herself to endure. She had been trained for that.

So she learned the comfort of routine, the accounts, the linen, the rules of calling, the soft tyranny of menus. Motherhood softened the sharpness of the days. Hattie's laughter pinned light to the walls. Theodore's frailty at birth frightened her and nursing him through those first weeks split something open in her, and dear Beatrice stepped into that break with a steadiness Georgina had never received from her own mother.

Now the small balance she had built felt newly precarious. The governess had done nothing wrong. And yet, from the first moment Florence had crossed the drawing-room threshold, Georgina had felt that subtle shift. Florence's restraint mirrored her own, but with a gravity that unsettled. It was like looking into still water and seeing her reflection tremble from a disturbance she could not name.

She rose and went to the window. The gardens lay drowned in mist; the fountain was no more than a shape. Beyond the lawns, lamps burned in the servants' range. Upstairs behind the nursery windows the fire would be sinking, and Florence would be a quiet figure in its light, speaking softly to a child already asleep.

A knock. A maid appeared to say it was past eleven. Georgina nodded. "Tell them I am coming." She remained a moment longer, looking at the glass. In the reflection her face appeared as it often did to herself, composed, a little severe, hair smooth as a promise.

"It is only that she is new," she told the reflection. "Strangers feel peculiar at first."

She turned. As the door closed, the fire lifted once, a last breath. The light fell back and the room accepted the dark.

. . .

Before sleep, Florence kept a habit. She moved through the nursery without noise, touching each small thing her pupils would wake to, like a book's worn spine, the corner of a blanket, the stub of a pencil left at the table. She opened the window a finger's breadth to let the room breathe. It calmed her, this ritual.

The corridor beyond lay empty, cool with stone and beeswax. From somewhere far in the house the tall clock sounded the quarter hour. She leaned her head against the nursery door and listened. Houses carried histories in their walls. Some chose to tell them. Branleigh, she thought, might be one of those.

She turned and sighed, weary from the day and sat in the rocking chair a moment longer than was necessary. When she finally rose, she slid the jar back within Hattie's reach. The burn-mark on the lid pressed a crescent against her palm. Heat without flame. Memory without picture.

"Another winter," she said again, barely a whisper, and let the room go to quiet.

3

The cherries came early that year; the bough above me dripped with white, as if spring carried its own snowfall. I spread my skirts on the grass and leaned against the moss-warmed sundial. Bees thrummed like a whisper while I began my letter. The paper trembled on my knee, not from cold but from the sweetness of thinking myself beloved. I wrote his name, William, and the ink seemed to remember him. I told him of the orchard in bloom, of the rook keeping watch from the elm, of the lambs crying in Mr Hatherley's pasture, of sounds so thin and hopeful they might be mistaken for angels if one were foolish or young. I told him I still kept the ribbon he'd tied around my wrist at Christmas, faded now, the knot worn from my fingers. I dared to imagine our rooms when he returned from barracks and the window facing east, the kettle singing, the small table for our bread. Not grand, but ours.

The garden moved in its quiet sermon of patience. Ants marched at the foot of the sundial, a robin pecked at the turned earth, the wall smelled of brick and thyme. Behind me, the house breathed with its curtains aired, a spoon chimed against a cup. Peace felt near enough to touch.

I had reached the tenderest part of my letter when my father's voice struck the air like iron. 'Where are you?' The pen blotted. My heart, obedient from habit, leapt like a pulled string. I folded the paper quickly and looked around with that instinct to hide that betrays both guilt and innocence. At the border where the grass met the rose-bed, I slipped the letter beneath a low branch, the thorn catching my glove. I freed myself, smoothed the soil, and a petal fell onto my wrist, like a white teardrop that would not melt. 'I am in the garden,' I called, steadying my voice.

He appeared a moment later, framed in the dark of the doorway, the black of his cassock making the light retreat. He came along the path, step even, expression calm as authority. 'Idleness,' he said. 'The enemy of souls.' He looked not at the cherries or bees or roses, but at me. 'Your time is not your own. Read the homilies, practise the hymns. Diligence brings favour.'

I rose at once. Obedience can move while a part of oneself remains seated in defiance. 'I'd finished my tasks for the morning,' I said. 'I wished to take the air.'

'The air,' he repeated, making the word small. 'You will find no profit in the air. Scripture says nothing of it.'

'Mother was pleased with my work, sir.'

'Your mother is too easily pleased.' He raised his hand, traced a cross in the space between us. 'Go in. Read. Pray.'

He left with his measured step, and the garden exhaled. I stood still until the latch clicked behind him. My hands were cold though the sun was kind. They came together by habit, a prayer formed without thought. 'I will read,' I said softly, 'and I will pray.' The robin scolded from the rose-bed, and I laughed, though the sound felt borrowed from someone else.

The day wore itself out properly. I sang the Psalm, stitched a hem until my fingers ached, answered my mother's questions, and avoided silence with my father. Yet the small pulse in the ground where my letter lay beat under my steps whenever I crossed the parlour. When the moon rose like a thin scythe harvesting the dark, I slipped out by the side door, shawl around my shoulders, breath held like contraband.

The garden at night belonged to another parish. The flowers kept counsel and the leaves grew still. Even the sundial seemed to measure different hours. The air smelled of damp brick and faint smoke. I knelt in the dew and parted the soil with care. The paper came up light, no heavier for its hiding. I brushed the dirt from the crease and held it to my chest. The moon made a pale doorway on the grass. The cherry bough stirred, letting fall a drift of white like a late blessing.

'He will come back,' I whispered. The night accepts truth and lies alike. 'He promised.' The word grew larger in the darkness, as if promise were alive, something to walk beside and feed with hope. I pressed the letter close until the paper warmed. For a moment I believed warmth could persuade the future.

When I returned, the house met me with its familiar creaks and warnings. A floorboard betrayed me as the clock gave a single chime. I closed my door gently and knelt by the bed. The letter lay under my palm like a talisman. I prayed as I had been taught, for guidance, wisdom, obedience. When those ended, my own words crept in, shy as beggars. Let him be safe. Let him think of me when the trumpet sounds at dawn. Let him come when the cherries are red. I do not know how Heaven measures such offerings, but when I rose it was not faith I felt most, but desire, a poor cousin to belief, yet never turned from the door.

I placed the letter beneath my pillow and lay awake, listening to the roof speak its slow, secret language. The moon climbed above the chimney-pots, casting the shadow of the cherry bough on my wall, trembling like a hand unsure whether to bless or strike. My father coughed somewhere in the house, dry, efficient, clearing the world. I closed my eyes and held William's promise between myself and the night, as if I could keep the page from turning. If I slept, it was into a place where gardens are always in blossom and no voice calls from the house to remind me that happiness is a labour for which I have not yet earned the tools.

4

The early days of Miss Marchwood's employment at Branleigh Park passed with a smoothness that might have satisfied the most exacting mistress. To an outsider, the household would have looked rebalanced, almost newly tuned. The children once given to sulks, sudden storms, and the small rebellions that gather in the corners of long afternoons were tractable. The nursery, accustomed to shawls carelessly slung and crumbs stitched into the carpet, took on an order that looked like peace and felt, to those who lived inside it, like something sterner.

Every object learned its place and kept it. Hattie's paint-box closed on clean wells and rinsed brushes laid in a straight line. Theodore's cradle stood at the same measured angle to the hearth, aligned as if some invisible compass lay under the floorboards and Miss Marchwood alone could read it. Even the light seemed to bend to her preference where it filtered through lace to fall in quiet bars across swept boards and polished chairs. Servants, respectful but cautious, lowered their whispers to barely heard when they passed. The nursery had become a small domain where order reigned without raising its voice.

Florence moved inside. Her step was quiet, but her presence

filled the air. When Hattie's temper surged as it did, reliably, in the manner of weather, Florence did not scold and instead she knelt. Her tone dropped until the child had to lean in to hear it. Rage dissolved not from fear but from attention, tears shrinking into a shy, relieved smile that always looked, to Georgina's eye, like surrender. With Theodore she was gentleness and precision. Soothed him so that his breathing settled, fed him so that the small muscles of his jaw unclenched, rocked him so he slept at the edge of waking and never fell hard into it. Theodore, restive even in his mother's arms, went quiet at the cool touch of the governess's hand and turned his face up in the wordless trust that only the very young can offer and the lonely recognise.

However, Lady Georgina, who could find no fault, found an ache instead. The perfection of Miss Marchwood's methods made her clumsy by contrast. The nursery had been the province of her affection and authority and now it felt like a stage where she performed in the wrong play. She would come in unannounced and find Hattie with her brows drawn down in work over a simple drawing or see her son reach for Florence's voice as if for the source of warmth itself, and what should have pleased her stung. It was not jealousy she told herself; it was caution, a mother's instinct to measure what she could not yet name.

On an afternoon of rain, the whole house had the sound of restraint about it. Firelight pulled the edges of the parlour closer, and damp rose from the bluebells in a jug on the centre table. Hattie, fresh from her gathering, had forgotten to remove her shoes. Across the pale carpet, a scatter of mud traced the exact path of delight to repentance. Georgina's morning had been needled with small vexations; patience tipped.

"Hattie." Her voice cracked the air. "How many times must I say it? Mud belongs in the garden, not the house. Look at your shoes then look at the floor."

The child froze, lips folding inward. Her eyes, sharp with a fox's instinct for where safety lies, went to Florence.

"She meant no harm, my lady," Florence said, already moving, the words soft enough to be a cushion. "I should have stopped her at the door."

The phrasing was gentle and exact: blame displayed, then removed. Georgina heard what sat beneath it, that mercy heals more than chastisement, and her neck tightened.

"You are kind to excuse her," she said, "but it is a mother's duty to correct as well as forgive."

"Of course, my lady." Florence inclined her head. She turned to Hattie, laid a hand on the tense small shoulder, and lowered her voice until the child's sobbing faltered to listen. "Your mama loves you very much and wishes to teach you good ways. We must not trouble her again, must we?"

The nod was wobbly but clear. Georgina had no second reprimand ready; none would fit that scene. She withdrew with the echo of the governess's tact following her down the corridor.

In the days that followed she tried to be sensible. Georgina made herself present for the ordinary things such as the measuring of a fever that did not amount to illness, the arrangement of little shoes beside one another like a row of habits, the selection of a book for evening that would not stir the child more than it soothed. But presence, she discovered, was not the same as use, and use was not the same as love. The more perfectly the nursery ran, the less certain she felt that it needed her.

That night, while the house slept and the corridor clocks agreed about the hour, the nursery kept its own time. The last coal folded into itself but Florence did not sleep. She sat with her hands folded and her gaze somewhere beyond the fireguard.

Serenity can be an appearance one offers to a room and it can also be a place one hides inside, where no one else is allowed to come.

She rose and stood before the washstand mirror. The glass was old and mottled, the sort that remembers former faces. It still returned hers as a pale steady oval, the mouth trained to gentleness, the eyes too bright for innocence. She studied the reflection with the same attention she gave to people she did not yet trust.

"Lady Florence Spencer," she whispered.

The name lived a moment on the air between truth and wish. She repeated it again, slower, letting the syllables land where they would. The second time it sounded less like a dream and more like a plan that had learned how to walk.

From the cradle a soft sound pulled her back. She went at once, pressed a finger lightly to the baby's lips, as if sealing a thought that should not be spoken. "Hush," she murmured. "All is well."

Her shadow, thrown long by the dying fire, crossed the floorboards and the figure on the wall did not look like a servant.

Lady Beatrice Spencer seldom invited anyone into her private sitting room. The chamber belonged to a life of quiet after a life of noise with shelves of books that had softened under long holding, drawers where embroidery floss lay in patient order, bowls of dried lavender that remembered last summer's heat. Watercolours on the walls had faded to gentler versions of themselves where Italy was remembered by someone who had not been able to stay. Through the tall south window, the garden kept its conversation with the weather. On a mild afternoon, with sunlight the colour of clean paper, she sent for Miss Marchwood to take tea.

Florence arrived without rush, the grey of her merino gown an answer to the room's restraint. Beatrice poured herself and was a habit that made the servants anxious and her calm as she observed her guest over the rim of the cup. Stillness at that age was rare. Georgina's had been learned, not innate.

"I trust you are settling," Beatrice said. "The country must seem dull after Cheltenham."

"Dullness can be a mercy, my lady," Florence replied. "It leaves time for thought."

Beatrice smiled at that. "Then you will be of interest to my son, though he is a man of action only in his imagination."

A flicker crossed the governess's face, perhaps amusement, or the idea of it. "I prefer observation to conversation," she said.

"Observation?" Beatrice tilted her head.

"Words are hospitable to disguise," Florence said. "Silence is less generous."

It was not piety and not exactly irreverence and it had the sound of someone who had watched other people long enough to know when their speech lied for them. Beatrice moved to ground that could not break, like the rhythm of the household, the children's progress, the ways a winter could thin a child's patience and a mother's temper at the same time. When she asked, gently, about Florence's family, the reply came without ornament.

"My parents are dead."

"I am sorry," Beatrice said. "Loss leaves questions only faith can answer."

"Faith answers what it chooses," Florence said. "Not always what we ask."

The older woman heard something like hunger in the even

tone. "You sound," she said, "as if sorrow has stayed longer than is polite."

The smile that answered her was small and private. "Most sorrows have excellent manners, my lady. They sit very quietly and never leave."

"You must forgive," Beatrice said, not sure for whose sake she said it. "Bitterness eats the very hand that feeds it."

For the first time the girl's control loosened at the edges. Her fingers tightened around the teacup, and her gaze went in, as if listening to something farther away than the room. When she spoke the words seemed to cool the air. "Sometimes forgiveness is the sin."

The clock ticked the same as before. Outside, a dove offered its soft, foolish prayer to the day. Beatrice heard her heartbeat argue once with her good sense.

"My dear," she said, gentler, "you have been hurt more than a heart is designed to bear."

"I am well now," Florence said. "The Lord heals all in time."

"He does," Beatrice said, and felt the lie inside the truth, "but sometimes He keeps His own pace."

When Florence had gone, the dowager sat at the window for a long time, watching the lawn grow longer in the glass. Mist lifted from the meadow. The yews held their shape against the dimming. The phrase, *forgiveness as sin*, stayed with her like an unfinished prayer. That evening Georgina came to bid Beatrice goodnight and heard more than she wished to when she asked after Florence.

"She is diligent," Beatrice said, "and there is something fastened inside her that won't come loose."

"You are too easily moved, Mama," Georgina answered. "Her refinement reads as rehearsal."

"Self-possession," Beatrice said, tired and not unkind, "can be a veil. It can also be a scar."

At this Georgina bridled and left the room swiftly leaving Beatrice alone and lost in deep thought. The name on her mind was that of the governess. While she pondered, from along the corridor came the faint deliberate notes of a piano, the melody careful as if the instrument were learning the room. The tune drifted and found Beatrice where she sat. It wavered between lullaby and lament, a thread of sound pulled out of another life. She listened until the final note thinned to nothing and discovered she had been holding her breath. Without meaning to, she crossed herself.

"God help her," she said. She could not say which *her* she meant.

All around her the household went to bed but Lady Beatrice did not. The clock in her room borrowed eleven from the hall and said it again to her. The fire collapsed into a bright pulse and then to memory. Lavender stayed in the air the way a familiar voice lingers in an empty room. She sat with her shawl tight and her thoughts unfastened.

Forgiveness as sin. The words did not accuse; they invited. Under their sound, old doors opened that she had kept politely closed. She had believed herself past the vanity of recollection. But time, like music, can be coaxed into returning. She remembered a younger self whose ease had not yet been trained out of her. And that girl she'd once been had come from Somerset, not Oxfordshire, with fields open as a sentence she had not learned to restrain, a father whose world was horses and harvests and the sturdy calm of money that did not speak about itself.

Her hair had been dark as wet chestnut, and her eyes (Henry had told her once, back when he still noticed anything but his own effort) had kept the sun even in shade. Her marriage had been a negotiation with civility. Henry Spencer needed sense wrapped in gentility and she required security that felt like stone. She had believed safety was a kind of love.

For a span of years the bargain worked exactly as bargains do even when it satisfied the letter and failed the spirit without anyone sensing the loss. The house prospered. A son grew. She played wife in the English manner and discovered that the role taught grace but not always kindness. Henry was a man of habits, not tenderness. Once he had won a thing, he set it on a shelf and dusted it when others called to see. Indifference, when it does not lift its hand to injure, is still a kind of cruelty when it wears love's face.

Silence taught her patience and patience taught her how to watch. She saw what longing did in others. The way a maid would linger near a forbidden smile and the way a groom stayed too long with a horse that did not need him. The way her son Charles became his father by practising the opposite and arrived, by that route, at the same place. Desire is a polite intruder. It comes in through doors marked duty and tidies the room after itself so no one thinks to check the silver.

When Henry died, she mourned without anguish. The candle went out with the economy she had always admired in him. A year of black taught her that peace and virtue often share a pew but pray different prayers in secret. She was forty-two and old in some ways and very young in others. Her joy, true, stubborn, difficult, lived in her son. Watching him was like watching a fine horse break to someone else's hand where all that beauty was harnessed to appetite. She had hoped Georgina might steady him. She had seen within weeks that the marriage met needs without touching souls.

Now, in the pattern of her days, she felt history bend back toward itself. A young woman had crossed her threshold with a beauty made quiet, secrets held as tight as a hand around a blade. Florence drew the gaze the way a wound draws the tongue to the broken tooth. Beatrice recognised peril and fascination and could not, if pressed, have said which was the greater.

She rose and went to the window. The night lay strict over Branleigh. The yews along the path made an honour guard for wildlife who cared not. The gravel showed a faint seam of light where the moon caught it. Beyond the trees her husband rested in the family vault, close enough to the roses to take their scent if the afterlife allowed.

Sometimes forgiveness is the sin. The phrase settled somewhere close to where prayer sits.

When she was younger, she had refused forgiveness once and called it justice. The memory came as if it had been waiting in that chair for her to sit. A maid, small, poor, frightened, had been caught trying to slip a brooch from Beatrice's dressing table into her apron pocket. The girl had wept and said her brother was ill and the price at the pawnbroker would buy medicine. Beatrice, stung by the insult of theft in her own room and the shame of her carelessness, had dismissed her without reference and taken the relief of tidy punishment as proof she had been right. She had never learned the girl's end. She had, however, learned, a year later that the brother's fever had been the end of him. For decades she told herself that mercy would have been weakness dressed as virtue. Tonight, with Florence's composed face and wounded words lifted up in her sight, that old argument crumbled like a thing left too long on a damp shelf. She pressed her palm to the glass and felt the pulse in her wrist argue with the cold.

Am I too late to forgive, she thought, *or did I never begin?*

Down the hall the faintest music began again. This time the melody came with fewer hesitations, as if the player had decided not to fear what could not be perfected. The tune was simple and sorrowful, the type a child might hum without knowing it's sad origins. Sound travelled through boards and plaster and bone until it seemed the house itself remembered something. She let her eyes close. It was not peace, the thing in the music. When the last note ended, the silence thickened into the kind found in chapels when everyone has gone and the stone keeps the prayers for later. She crossed herself a second time. She did not choose a name for the soul she meant. Her own. Her son's. The young woman's. It is a habit of older hearts to pray in plural.

In the nursery, order held, even in sleep. Florence walked the small room and set Hattie's doll upright on its chair, turned a book face-down so the child would find it the moment she woke, placed the blanket so that Theodore's kick would not bare him to the air. She paused by the window and opened it the width of a coin to let the night breathe the day out. She touched the piano with her fingertips rather than her hand and closed the fall as if laying a secret back into its box. In the ash of the grate a faint loop of scorched thread marked where something had once smouldered and gone out. She pressed the toe of her shoe to it and erased the sign.

When she lay down at last, she did not sleep quickly. The edges of the day shuffled through her mind and tried to reorder themselves. The scene in the parlour replayed without sound and then with it, her name on Beatrice's tongue returned without judgement and then with it, and a memory older than Branleigh came uninvited: a cold church, a father's hand raised not in blessing but in the gesture that clears the air of what does not please it. She turned her face to the wall and let the thought pass. Thoughts that are not yet useful should be kept, like letters that have not been answered, somewhere safe and out of sight.

. . .

Georgina slept and woke and slept again, the way a mind does when it is training itself not to think the obvious thought. In the morning she went to the nursery early and found only ordinary devotion. Hattie, hair a tangle of impatience, sat for plaiting with a martyr's sigh. Theodore lay round and content on a folded blanket while Florence counted out soft claps to match his kicks. Nothing was wrong. Nothing invited fear. The very simplicity of the scene made the small bruise inside her deepen.

"Good morning, Mama," Hattie said, and held out the ribbon she had chosen, as if the choice might make a difference to the way love worked in the world.

Georgina took the ribbon and threaded it, hands steady. "This colour suits you," she said.

"It suits Hector, too," Hattie said, and produced the jam-jar from beneath her chair, the snail within conducting its slow tour of the glass. "He thinks it makes him brave."

"Does he?" Georgina said. Her voice did not betray the way the morning was breaking inside her, quietly, tidily, the way ice gives up underfoot, with no drama and all the danger.

Florence looked up, and whatever lay between them, the question neither had admitted, passed like a cool hand across a fevered brow. No word for it, and so no quarrel yet.

After the lessons, Georgina lingered and made herself useful with small nonsense such as counting the buttons that needed replacing, sorting the faded ribbons to one side of the drawer and the bright to the other, pretending decisions mattered when the only decision that weighed anything refused to declare itself. As she left, the governess said her name without title. Georgina paused. The single syllable sounded neither bold nor wrong.

"Lady Georgina," Florence corrected herself at once.

Georgina turned, prepared to say the polite thing. The words went astray. "Yes," she said, and found that it answered more than the correction.

. . .

By afternoon the rain lightened, and the smell of wet stone left the corridors. Charles crossed the hall with a purposeful gait that convinced no one, as his purposeful gaits never did. He glanced toward the drawing room as he passed and saw, at the far end, the small piano no one played. He lifted the fall and pressed one key, as if testing whether the instrument could be relied on to do what was asked of it. The note was a little flat. He smiled as if the fault were part of its charm.

In the evening he drifted where light and conversation gathered. He half-read the paper, half-watched his wife work through correspondence, half-listened to his mother's measured comments on parish matters that were not his concern. He was a man composed of halves, each convincing on its own. When a footman carried a tray toward the nursery with milk and a small plate, Charles followed the direction of travel with his eyes only. He said nothing at all.

Beatrice saw the glance and said nothing either. The old wisdom returned: there are moments when speaking turns suspicion into fact.

That night the melody did not come. The silence had its own depth. Beatrice felt it and decided not to visit it with thoughts. She went to bed with the deliberate motions of someone who has lived long enough to know that most questions are made worse by midnight.

In the nursery the window remained the width of a coin. The air cooled and clarified. In her bed, Hattie slept with one hand open, as if she had been given a thing and wanted to keep enough space for more. The baby breathed even and deep.

Florence lay awake and counted the clock's quarter. When at last sleep came, it came with no images attached.

Morning began again, as mornings do in houses that pride themselves on the predictability of breakfast and the moral tedium of punctuality. The rhythm was the same. It felt different only to those who had started listening.

The nursery door stood open an inch. A servant hovered to ask whether Hattie's pinafores should be mended with the finer thread or the cheaper. Georgina answered and did not later remember what she had chosen. Beatrice wrote a note to the Society for the Relief of Prisoners' Families and did not send it. Charles whistled half a tune he had not learned. The house continued. Order kept order.

By the week's end, nothing had happened that could be reported. The children improved in small measurable ways that made servants nod in corridors. The nursery maintained its polish. The perfect angle of the cradle held. The governess's stillness did not crack. Georgina's unease did not name itself. Beatrice prayed, once, without words and considered that perhaps she had been doing that all her life.

In the quiet between breakfast and bed, when most people's lives declare themselves without their knowing it, a soundless decision was made in more than one heart. To wait, to watch, to forgive later, to forgive never, to stay, to wish, to act, and to call each of those choices by another name until the house itself insisted on the truth.

5

In every great house there is a corner where quiet gathers thickest; at Branleigh Park it was the nursery at first light, before the fire was laid and while the mist pressed its cold cheek to the windowpanes. There Annie Larkin, the wet nurse, began her day. She was twenty-three, small and pale, a gentleness about her that seemed to apologise for existing. Her eyes were the thin blue of skimmed milk, her hair soft as straw, her voice seldom above a whisper. She moved with the care of one long unaccustomed to gratitude, and yet there was reverence in her slowness, as if every task passed through a hidden wound before it reached her hands.

Among the servants her story was known or at least embroidered into something that resembled truth. She had once been a laundress in the village; she had loved unwisely; and when her belly rose the father vanished like mist on a summer morning. The workhouse took her in. The baby, once born, was taken from her in turn. She tried to see him again, they said, and found his name already struck from the register, his little body buried in a pauper's plot. Whatever the facts, the grief was plain. Each evening, when her duties were done, she walked to the church in Branleigh village to light a single candle in the Lady Chapel. The cook who was fond of sad tales had said it was for the child's soul but the footman declared no good Christian should pray for the dead of uncertain birth.

When Florence Marchwood entered the household, she found Annie already installed in the nursery, her place defined by silence and service. The governess greeted her with that soft civility which makes even kindness sound deliberate. For several days they spoke only of the children's needs, the hours of feeding, the quantity of milk, Lady Georgina's regimen, until one afternoon Florence lingered by the window seat where Annie rocked the baby. Late spring light sifted through muslin, touching the child's downy head and the nurse's bowed face.

"You have a gift with infants," Florence said. "He thrives with you."

Annie looked up, uncertain whether the remark was praise or inquiry. "He's a good little thing, miss," she said simply. "Hardly cries unless the wind's sharp. I'm fortunate, that's all."

"Fortunate," Florence repeated, tasting the word. "Some would say blessed."

Annie smiled faintly but did not answer. Florence's tone remained light, conversational. "You have no family of your own, Mrs Larkin?"

"No, miss," Annie said, barely audible. "None I can speak of."

Florence watched her a moment longer. "How did you come to service, if I may ask?"

So softly put, yet the question struck a hidden nerve. Annie's eyes filled before she could turn away. "It was the only place left," she whispered. "After... after my trouble. They said I should be grateful for honest work. And I am, miss, I am. Only..."

Her words broke. The baby stirred at her breast, searching.

She adjusted her shawl, pressed him close, and murmured, "There now, my darling."

"Only what?" Florence asked, gently.

Annie swallowed. "Only that I think of my own when I hold him."

Silence followed save for the tick of the clock, the faint crackle of the hearth, the steady rhythm of feeding. Florence did not move her gaze from the child. Her expression showed sympathy, yet her stillness had other meaning as though she listened not to Annie, but to a voice that lived just behind her own. When she spoke again her tone was measured and far away. "A mother's heart remembers, whatever the world decrees. Take comfort in that."

Annie nodded, though uneasily. Something in the governess was too composed, too intent and it disturbed her. She shifted the baby and turned aside under pretext of straightening his blanket. Florence kept watching, her eyes fixed with a concentration so fierce it looked like reverence.

That evening, when the lamps were lowered and Annie had gone down to supper, Florence stayed in the nursery under pretence of finishing a letter. The cradle stood by the fire, curtains half drawn and within, the infant slept, breath rising and falling with regular grace. Florence set down her pen and crossed the room. She stood looking for a long moment, the fire's glow warming her pallor. One gloved hand reached out, fingers resting lightly on the carved cradle-rail.

"Mine," she whispered. Barely a breath, yet in the hush it carried the force of prayer, or curse.

Behind Florence the door opened a fraction. Lady Georgina stood on the threshold, unseen. She had come to check the children before retiring and at the sight of the governess bending over the cradle she hesitated. Something in Florence's attitude, the bowed head, the devotional stillness, gave her pause. She drew back and closed the door silently, rebuking herself for intrusion.

Later, undressing by her own fire, Georgina thought of nurse and governess, two women of the lower sort, bound by a child that belonged to neither. In recent days she had noticed a new tautness between them, stiffness, half-wary glances. She told herself it was nothing; servants, like hounds, were prone to jealousy. Among such women, the hierarchies of motherhood and society could never be simple.

Satisfied with this explanation, she opened her prayer book. The words blurred. Into the page stole the image she had not invited, the cradle, the firelight, a hand resting on wood as on an altar. She could not have said why it unsettled her.

Evening settled over Branleigh Park and the rain, long threatening, began at last to fall in slanting threads that glimmered like spun glass against the panes. Lamps were lit in the drawing room; the family gathered as custom required before supper. The air held the faint, over-sweet scent of roses brought in from the conservatory, a fragrance already turning toward decay.

Lady Georgina sat with her embroidery, posture immaculate, lamplight striking pale gold from her rings. Her husband stood by the mantel, one hand resting on the marble, his gaze wandering from the fire to the door, where Florence entered to return a book of the Dowager's. Florence curtseyed, murmuring something about Lady Beatrice's health. The softened light made an almost spectral beauty of her; the plain grey dress seemed to take and return the lamp like silver. She set the volume on a side table. A small pause followed, one of those house-moments when fault lines show if anyone looks.

"You are a marvel with the children, Miss Marchwood,"

Charles said, breaking the hush. Warm, unstudied. "I've not seen Theodore so content since his christening. Georgina tells me he scarcely wakes."

Florence inclined her head. "I am grateful to serve, my lord. The children are blessings, each in their way."

"Indeed," he smiled. "You must have a saint's patience."

"Patience, my lord," she said gently, "is a habit one acquires by necessity."

Innocent words, yet they landed with a thud that Georgina felt. She looked up, needle suspended mid-stitch. "We are fortunate to have found someone so devoted," she said; correct, cool.

Charles turned to her. "You might rest a little yourself, my dear. You've worn yourself thin with the little ones. It's good to have help."

"I manage well enough," she answered at once. The thin smile did not reach her eyes.

Sensing the tension she had not meant or had meant too precisely, Florence curtseyed again. "If you'll excuse me, my lady, I must settle the children."

Her skirts whispered across the carpet like a secret leaving the room and when she was gone the quiet pressed in. Georgina stared at her embroidery, needle still. The rain tapped at the glass like someone begging admission.

Charles stirred the fire as if it needed tending; his expression had become thoughtful. "She has a rare composure," he said at last. "Not many women or her station possess such calm."

"Perhaps," Georgina replied without looking up, "because she has fewer things to lose."

He frowned, unsure if he heard terseness or fatigue. "You're overtired, Georgina. You find cracks where there are none."

"Perhaps," she said again, but there was no conviction in it.

Later, alone at her dressing table, she sat while her maid

brushed out her hair. The mirror showed a face too still, too pale. Candlelight was an unforgiving companion to women past first youth and revealed what she had not wished to see. Faint lines at the eyes, the delicate tracery of worry and restraint. The startle she felt was not vanity but the proof that time moves on while one is busy holding appearances steady. Leaning closer, she thought, So this is how it begins.

Dismissed at last, the maid withdrew. Georgina remained, studying herself until the candle dimmed. Behind her, the old house creaked into night under the slow symphony of timbers and sighs it knew by heart.

In the nursery, another quiet reigned. The fire burnt low while curtains were drawn against the rain. Florence sat beside the cradle, gown catching and releasing the flame's flicker as she rocked with one hand. Her lips moved, forming words too soft to distinguish; the tune that threaded them was clear yet low and slow, strange as prayer.

She bent over the sleeping child. "Your mother is tired and needs peace," she whispered, voice soft, almost tender. "I shall keep you safe."

The infant stirred and sighed, then settled, tiny fingers curling in the lace. Florence watched a long while, unblinking, as if willing his chest to rise and fall in time with her own.

Outside, the rain thickened. It ran down the panes in narrow silver streams and blurred the reflection of the woman by the cradle until her face seemed to merge with the darkness behind her.

The lullaby went on, hardly more than breath yet the same refrain repeating. When at last the fire fell to ash, the house exhaled as if relieved to sleep. And still, within the nursery, the whispering continued.

6

The room smelled of vinegar and fear. I remember the two scents twisting together, sharp and sour, until they filled my mouth whenever I tried to breathe. The walls of the rectory had never seemed close before that week, but they pressed upon me then like the lid of a box meant for something no longer alive. The curtains were drawn to keep the light from my eyes, though it was not the light that pained me. I lay still, my body one great bruise, and tried to believe what my mother whispered, that pain is passing and the Lord's mercy everlasting. But mercy leaked out of me hour by hour, and none returned.

Downstairs, my father's voice rose and fell in its familiar rhythm, measured, faultless, each phrase polished by years of preaching. Forgiveness, he said, is the highest act of love. The words thudded up through the floorboards and struck me like the echo of his hand the night before, when he had called my shame a scourge to be beaten out. His sermon had not changed: the same conviction, the same hollow faith. I pressed my palms over my ears, but his voice seeped through my skin like water through cloth. Forgive. Obey. Repent. Each word was a hammer on stone.

My mother came to me in those intervals when the house slept.

She carried broth I could not swallow and damp cloths for my brow. Her hands trembled as she touched me, as though pity itself might be overheard. When she wept, she did it silently, the tears sliding down her cheeks as she wiped the blood from mine. We were conspirators in disgrace, and the knowledge of it aged her. Once she whispered she would send for the doctor but my father must never know. I told her it was too late for doctors. I already knew what was coming. The child within me was too still, too silent.

When the pain began, it was not sharp but wide like a fire spreading through hollow ground. I clutched at the sheet until it tore beneath my nails. The hours blurred, measured only by the creak of floorboards as my mother paced, and by my father's voice once more below, reading the evening prayers with perfect calm. He did not falter when my cry broke the stillness. He did not come.

The doctor arrived at last, summoned in secret haste. His boots tracked mud across the rug; his hands smelled faintly of tobacco and sulphur. He looked at me once and said nothing. When the small weight slipped from me into the world, it made no sound. I saw the doctor's face that showed not pity, not sorrow, only the fatigue of one who has seen too many losses to name them tragedy. He turned to my mother, spoke low, then packed his bag and left, closing the door gently, as if silence could undo what had happened.

My mother stayed beside me until dawn. The candle burned low as she held the bundle to her breast for a moment, then wrapped it tighter, her lips moving in a prayer I could not hear. She thought me asleep when she carried the small body from the room. I did not speak. I could not. Only the scent of linen and milk remained and the faint ghost of life that lingers after it is gone. When I woke again, the cradle beside my bed was empty, the blanket folded as neatly as a church cloth after service.

I remember the moment I understood. The hollow at my side where the bundle had been grew endless. I called his name though I had not yet chosen one, and the sound came from some place deeper than speech, half cry, half prayer. They locked the door to keep me from following. Through the panel I heard my mother's sobs, and beyond the window, the scrape of spades biting earth. She buried him at the edge of the churchyard, where nettles grow and the ground never dries. There is no marker there, only grass. I did not see it. I was not permitted.

They said I raved for days. Perhaps I did. Fever has a way of making sense of things that sanity cannot. I only know that when the fever broke, the world returned bleak and terrible. I lay still so they would think me healed, but inside I listened to the wind through the chimney, to the sigh of the dying fire, to every small cry the night invents when the living have fallen silent. One evening I heard him. My child. The sound was faint, high, drawn through air as if through water. They said it was the wind. My father said I must not blaspheme. But I knew that voice. I had carried it beneath my ribs; I had heard it in dreams before he was born. They buried him alive.

After that I stopped speaking to anyone but the dark. They called it fever again, though it felt like waking from a long deceit. Between the dreams I felt the warmth of a small hand against mine, a whisper at my ear too soft for others to hear. When they found me smiling, they said it was madness. But I knew it was forgiveness. In that touch, in that imagined breath, he told me he understood. That it was not my fault. The rest is blurred, the doctor's return, the white sheets turned red, my mother's broken prayers. I remember only that finally I slept, and in sleep he stayed near.

Years have passed, and still I hear him. The sound has softened but not gone, like a church bell smothered by distance. He calls when the wind rises, and I answer as mothers do, with tears. But tonight, as I drift once more into the dark, I tell him to hush. Hush, little one. Hush now. Your mother is here. Your mother never left.

7

The long summer had settled over Branleigh Park like a spell. Even at midnight the air lay thick and breath-warm, and the scent of roses drifted through open windows, sweet enough to suffocate. The house slept and its corridors exhaled the slow rhythm of the dark. Only the clocks kept time, patient and relentless.

In the small chamber adjoining the nursery, Florence Marchwood stirred from uneasy dreams. Her nightdress clung damply to her skin while her breath came short, as if she had been running. The candle she had left for comfort had melted to a trembling ring of wax. She lay still and listened. The silence intensified until she could hear the faint pulse in her ears. Then it came again, soft, uncertain, unmistakable. An infant's cry.

Not Theodore. She knew his thread of sound the way one knows the shape of one's name in a crowded room. This was deeper, distant, and edged with that pleading tone that belongs to memory more than to breath. Florence sat up, hair stuck to her temples, eyes wide to the dark. The cry returned, fainter, borne from somewhere below the window. Without thinking, she rose. Bare feet made no sound on the boards. Moonlight, filtered through a narrow gap in the curtain, cut a pale path across the floor.

She drew the fabric aside. The lawn lay silvered, blades of grass glinting as if made of glass. Beyond the great cedar, the rose garden stretched in neat dark rows, blooms closed like hands in prayer. The stillness looked perfect and then wavered. Something moved among the flowers: a slight quiver, too deliberate for wind, too small for a person. The cry rose once more. Clearer. Nearer.

Recognition shivered through her, not fear, but that aching shock with which a name returns too late. She reached for her shawl and her hands shook as she gathered it tight around her. The corridor clock struck twelve as the chapel bell answered, deep and solemn, vibrations passing through her bones. That sound always chilled her; she did not examine why.

Moments later she slipped down the servants' stair. The house slept on and no board protested. Air cooled as she crossed the scullery, stone flags damp beneath her soles. She lifted the latch, stepped into the night, and the dew took her feet in cold, shining kisses.

Across the lawn, the roses breathed their wine-thick scent. She paused at the garden's edge, breath small in the silver air. "I'm here," she whispered. "My darling, I've come back."

Her words dissolved then a sigh seemed to answer, a rustle against petals, a stirring that might have been wind, or something gentler. She sank to her knees among the roses. Thorns grazed her palms. "Hush now," she murmured. "I will find you. I will not leave you again."

The chapel bell tolled once, slow, singular. Its echo held while she bowed her head and wept, tears spattering the soil like rain recalled from a kinder season. Dawn restored the ordinary. Servants moved through their rounds with the quiet confidence of habit. In the nursery, Annie Larkin noticed a trail of small dark prints leading from the open window to the cradle. Bare feet, a woman's size, stamped in the thin ash that had escaped from the grate. Annie scolded the housemaid for negligence and wiped the marks away.

Florence appeared soon after, hair neatly pinned, face composed to serenity. When Annie mentioned the prints, she listened without a flicker.

"It was a dream," she said. "I thought I heard him crying."

"The baby, miss?"

Florence's eyes trembled, but no more than a breath of a change and a faint smile touched her mouth. "Yes. The baby."

She took Theodore in her arms and kissed his brow. "He sleeps so soundly, doesn't he?"

Annie nodded, uneasy without knowing why, and let the matter fall where countless small matters fall in large houses, into silence.

At breakfast the family gathered as usual. Conversation drifted: weather, rose harvest, the vicar's proposed call. Hattie, half-listening, swung her legs and hummed.

"What is that tune, dear?" Georgina asked.

"The one Miss Florence sings to baby," Hattie said, pleased. "Sleep beneath the roses, child."

Georgina stilled. "What did you say?"

"The song, Mama. *Sleep beneath the roses.*"

The words hung, simple and dreadful. Georgina glanced at Charles. He laughed, lightly, with unease pooled beneath.

"What an odd little rhyme," he said. "You must have dreamt it."

But Georgina knew she had taught no such song. When she looked toward the governess, she found Florence already watching her, eyes lowered, mouth curved in a small, secret smile. Outside, the roses nodded in a breath of morning wind. Across the valley the chapel bell spoke once and was quiet.

. . .

By the next day the air had turned oppressive again, pressing low as if thunder crouched just out of sight. The house moved as though beneath glass, it's sounds muted, gestures careful. Even the children were subdued.

Lady Beatrice Spencer noticed first. Florence came to the morning room to fetch a book of hymns. The composure was in place, but her skin had taken on the transparency of the overtired and her hands trembled when she lifted the teacup Beatrice offered.

"My dear," the Dowager said gently, "you look unwell. Have you been overexerting yourself?"

Florence smiled too quickly and set the cup down before its rim could betray a clink. "Not at all, my lady. I have never felt more alive."

The mild words, delivered with serene conviction, ran cold along Beatrice's spine as she noticed that Florence's pupils were wide in the morning light and a feverish bloom touched her cheeks. Yet when Beatrice met her eye, there was no embarrassment only a quiet certainty that discouraged further questions.

"You must rest," Beatrice said, schooling her voice. "Even innocent duties can weary the spirit."

"I find rest in my duties," Florence replied. "And peace near the children."

She curtseyed with infallible grace and withdrew, leaving Beatrice troubled by the brightness of her smile which was too intense, as if lit from within by a flame not wholly under command.

That afternoon, while heat thickened and the roses drooped against the wall, Beatrice sought Georgina in her sitting room.

She found her bent over correspondence, concentration drawn thin.

"My dear," Beatrice said, waiting until the last seal was pressed, "I wish you would keep a closer eye on your governess."

"Miss Marchwood?" Georgina's surprise was mild. "She requires no supervision. The children adore her. Even the servants say she has a gift."

"A gift can be dangerous when the giver does not understand its cost," Beatrice said. "The woman looks haunted to me, restless, as if she has left something unfinished behind her."

"You are fanciful, Mama," Georgina said with indulgence. "Heat makes weary of us all. A touch more sleep and she'll be herself."

Beatrice sighed, unwilling to press and unable to let go. "I have lived long enough to recognise a troubled spirit."

Georgina turned back to her papers. "She works too hard. That is all."

But even as she spoke, a sliver of memory slid under the door of her denial: that morning she had paused outside the nursery and heard Florence's voice, lower than usual, rhythmic, almost a prayer. Cold had run lightly over her skin; she had blamed a draft. "You worry too much, Mama," she said, firmer. "All is well."

Beatrice allowed the conversation to end, carrying her unease back to her room, where it settled on her like the heaviness of the weather.

In the nursery the air held the scent of warm linen and a child's sweet milk breath. Florence moved in silence, tidying what needed no tidying, arranging the small world to her design, brushes aligned, ribbons sorted, a book turned face down so the first page would meet the child's eyes at morning. At last she stopped beside the cradle. Theodore lay sleeping, fists curved against his chest, mouth slack in perfect peace. Florence knelt. Her face was expressionless, her breathing shallow.

"She doesn't love you as I do," she whispered.

Her hand hovered, trembled, withdrew, folded hard into her lap. "No one ever will."

The baby stirred, parted his lips as though to answer, and drifted deeper instead. Florence's mouth softened. She began to hum the tune that had haunted her sleep, the lullaby with its petals and its promise of rest. Outside, thunder muttered beyond the hills, a low preface to storm. Inside, the nursery held its breath. Peace stretched thin as blown glass, and the faintest breath might have shattered it.

8

The late days of June laid a languid heat over Branleigh Park. Even the bees moved heavily among the lavender, their droning a tired vibration that held the afternoons in a stupor. In the nursery the air was closer still, the curtains half-drawn, the faint sourness of milk, the relentless waft of roses through the open casement.

Annie Larkin worked quietly at her mending, the baby sleeping in his cradle beside her. Now and then she glanced toward Miss Marchwood, who sat by the window with a book unopened in her lap, her gaze lowered to the gardens. The governess looked composed, yet lately Annie had learned to see the strain in that stillness and the way peace can be worn like a garment that pinches at the seams.

A week had passed since Hattie, in the offhand cruelty of innocence, had chattered while Florence was below stairs. *"Miss Florence kissed baby's feet and called him her heaven's gift. Isn't that funny, Nurse? Mama never does that."* Annie had laughed then, hollow to her own ear. The image would not leave her, though, a woman bent over a cradle, lips to tiny feet, words spoken like a prayer. Harmless, perhaps. And yet in her imagination the tenderness was unguarded and too intense to be ordinary.

Watching Florence's profile against the evening, unease crept back like tide reclaiming the shore. What had seemed angelic now looked too polished, its marble smoothness concealing fault-lines beneath.

"Miss," Annie ventured at last, "you'll spoil your eyes, sitting so long without a candle."

Florence turned, slowly. "I wasn't reading," she said. "Only thinking."

"About what, miss, if I may?"

A faint smile came and went. "Many things, Mrs Larkin. We all have our thoughts, don't we?"

Polite, and no comfort. Annie bent again to her stitching; the needle wavered in her fingers. "I think about the little one I lost," she said softly, almost to herself. "When I hold him" she glanced at the sleeping child, "I can't help but think of mine. It's a blessing, and a sorrow."

Florence looked at her with an expression that might have been sympathy or assessment. "Some souls," she said, "come only to remind us of what heaven sounds like when it shuts its doors."

Annie frowned. "That's a sad thing to say, miss."

"The truth often is."

Heat thickened the silence. The hairs rose at Annie's nape. "You've seen sorrow yourself, haven't you?" she asked gently, steering toward safer ground. "I can tell. Sometimes I wonder what brought you here."

Florence's gaze drifted to the window. "The Lord orders our steps," she said. "We needn't question the road."

"I mean before Branleigh," Annie persisted, still soft. "You've never spoken of your people."

"My family," Florence repeated, even, distant. "There is little to tell. The past is a book best shut, Mrs Larkin. Too many ghosts press at the margins."

Annie swallowed. "It must be lonely, having no one."

"I am never lonely," the governess said. Her eyes stayed on the hedgerows where the last light bled away. "Some do not leave us, even when they're gone."

The gentle words carried weight; Annie shivered. She folded her mending. "I'll fetch fresh water," she said, eager to break the hush.

"Thank you," Florence murmured. "You are very kind."

Annie gathered her workbasket and left. As she went down the back stair a sound drifted after her, a humming, slow and mournful, threaded with a sweetness that made her skin prickle. She paused and it ceased at once. She hurried on, hands trembling before she reached the servants' hall, and blamed the heat.

It began, as such terrors do, with small things. A comb out of place. A folded apron no longer where it had been left. A pitcher half-emptied that no one owned to using. At first Annie blamed herself. The room was warm; weariness makes fools of us. But unease gathered, clinging to the walls the way milk sours the air.

She avoided Miss Marchwood when she could. The governess's calm rattled her. It was the unnatural completeness of it. When they met, Florence's politeness was *too* perfect and her gaze lingered a heartbeat longer than courtesy allowed. Annie found reasons to tarry in the laundry, drew water from the well herself, counted and recounted the nursery linen as if number might steady her. Nothing checked the creeping dread.

One morning she woke to find her basket overturned, thread unspooled across the floor like pale silk. The window latch stood open though she remembered closing it. Later, her rosary was gone from the shelf beside her bed, a cheap thing, wooden beads darkened by years of prayer and its absence left her breathless, as if the small comfort had anchored her to something steady.

She searched, fingers shaking. Miss Marchwood glided in, unhurried.

"You've lost something, Mrs Larkin?"

"My rosary," Annie said. "It was here last night. I can't think... "

Florence bent without haste and reached beneath the cradle. When she rose, the beads hung from her fingers. "Is this it?" she asked, smiling. "You must have dropped it, poor thing."

Annie stared. "I... yes. But how?"

She took it, grateful and cold. Had she truly been so careless? The thought chilled.

"You mustn't worry," Florence said softly. "Sleep plays tricks when one is overtired. These little mistakes mean nothing."

The voice soothed and unsettled together. Annie nodded. "Yes, miss."

When the governess left, she sank to the chair, the beads cutting her palm, and tried to pray. The words failed.

By week's end the servants whispered. Mary the scullery maid swore she'd seen the governess slip along the corridor after midnight, her gown pale as smoke. The housemaid claimed she heard singing from the nursery long after lights were doused, a slow, lilting melody, neither hymn nor lullaby but something between. The tales grew with the telling, as tales will. One evening, when Georgina descended with a recipe for the cook, she heard the talk. It died the moment her shadow crossed the threshold as faces bent to work. She dismissed it as boredom's froth but the unease clung as she climbed the stair.

Passing the nursery, she paused. The door stood ajar. Lamplight wavered but her daughter's voice carried.

"Say it again, Miss Florence," Hattie pleaded. "Say it the way you do at bedtime."

"Hush, sweetheart," came the governess's voice, tender, firm. "It's time for sleep."

"But I want to hear it, please, *Mama*."

The name struck Georgina hard. She stepped inside. "Hattie!"

The child flinched. "I meant Miss Florence... "

"Do not call your governess *Mama*," Georgina said. "That is a name you have no right to give away."

Hattie's lip trembled. She looked to Florence, who stood very still by the crib, face pale in the flame's tremor.

"It was my fault, my lady," Florence said at once, humble and soft. "The child was playing, that is all. Please don't be angry with her."

The humility needled Georgina's irritation. "Children repeat what they hear," she said. "It would be wiser to guard your speech."

Florence bowed her head. "You are quite right. Forgive me."

Her eyes glistened, not with tears, Georgina thought, but with something like triumph. Or perhaps only lamplight.

She turned away before the thought could form, drew her daughter close, kissed her goodnight, and left.

When the door closed, Florence lingered at the cradle. Hattie's little sobs thinned to hiccups; the baby turned and sighed in sleep. The governess looked down at them both, unreadable.

"Children speak truth more often than their elders," she murmured. "They name what is."

Her hand rested on the rail; the curve of her mouth suggested the ghost of a smile.

Outside, thunder rolled faintly over the fields, and the old house seemed to listen.

Dinner that evening unfolded beneath a veil of tension so fine that every movement threatened to tear it. The air was thick under the chandelier; candles burned low and slow, their wavering light softening the edges of the table's silver and glass. Outside, the storm that had broken before dusk still breathed against the windows, warm, damp, carrying the scent of wet roses through every door a servant opened.

Lady Georgina sat at the head of the table, her spine straight as habit, her complexion pale beneath the shimmer of the candelabra. She lifted her fork and lowered it with mechanical grace, tasting nothing. Opposite her, Lord Charles seemed untouched by the heaviness that lay over the room. He was animated, restored by food and wine, and wholly untroubled by his wife's silence.

"You've been sharp these past few days, Georgina," he said lightly, setting down his glass. "One might think you've taken a dislike to our new governess. Poor woman can hardly draw breath without your inspection."

Georgina looked up, eyes bright though her expression remained composed. "I have no complaint about Miss Marchwood's performance," she said evenly. "Only her influence. The children are impressionable."

"Influence?" His smile deepened. "She's devoted to them, that's all, such a treasure in her line of work. You should be grateful, my dear; you've been spared a great deal of trouble."

The words struck her like silk drawn over a blade. "A mother requires no rival in her own house."

Charles laughed softly. "A rival? Really, Georgina, you make her sound like some heroine in a French romance. She's a governess, not a temptress."

At the far end of the table, Lady Beatrice lifted her eyes from her plate. The lamplight touched her silver hair, framing her face with the melancholy dignity of an old portrait. She said nothing, only observed her son with the quiet, piercing gaze of one who has seen men mistake self-assurance for wisdom.

Charles, too sure of his charm to notice, poured himself more wine. "You're out of sorts, that's all," he went on. "The heat, the children, perhaps fatigue. Miss Marchwood's devotion is nothing but kindness."

Georgina's hand trembled as she set down her glass. "You mistake composure for kindness," she said. "There's something unnatural in her serenity. She watches everything and listens when no one speaks."

Charles chuckled. "Good heavens, Georgina, you sound like the maids with their ghost stories. Shall I forbid her to sing lullabies next?"

Beatrice's voice, low but steady, cut through the laughter. "Charles," she said, "a wise man does not laugh at his wife's instincts."

He turned toward her, surprised. "Surely you don't share these fancies, Mother?"

Her gaze did not waver. "No. But I've lived long enough to see how easily men mistake fascination for virtue."

The words landed softly, like pebbles dropped into deep water, but their ripples reached every corner of the table. The candle flames seemed to falter in the pause that followed as Charles flushed, part embarrassment, part resentment.

"You're all determined to turn the woman into a ghost," he said. "I'll not join the séance."

No one replied. The rest of the meal passed in brittle silence, the kind that prickles with things unsaid. When the table was cleared and the family rose, Beatrice lingered at the doorway. She watched her son follow his wife upstairs, his hand light on Georgina's shoulder, her face turned from him. The sight drew an ache she had thought long extinguished. It summoned another dining room, another silence, another husband whose charm had been armour, whose blindness had worn the same easy smile.

Later, the house sank into its nocturnal hush. A faint wind lifted the curtains, stirring them like guests unsure of their welcome. Along the corridor, Florence Marchwood moved without sound, the hem of her gown whispering over the boards. She paused beside the half-open door of the master bedroom, her head slightly inclined.

Voices reached her, muffled but distinct. Georgina's, tight with anger; Charles's, soft and defensive.

"You defend her at every turn," Georgina said. "Do you not see how the servants look at her? How she presumes upon your attention?"

"I see a woman who performs her duties faultlessly," Charles replied. "If you choose to imagine grievances, I cannot help it."

A chair scraped sharply against the floor, followed by silence.

Florence's lips curved. She waited a moment longer, the faintest light from the hall striking her cheek. Then she turned away, pressing a hand to her chest as though to quiet the quick, fluttering beat beneath.

"He'll choose me," she whispered in words so low they seemed to form from breath rather than speech.

Then she smiled, a small, secret smile and glided down the corridor toward the nursery, where two children slept and the air still carried the faint perfume of roses and rain.

9

The first thing one learns in such a place is the weight of air. At Ravenbrooke, it was not breathed but borne, a thickness salted with carbolic and something older, flatter, as though despair itself had a scent that could be scrubbed but never erased. The corridors narrowed the farther one walked, the walls closing like hands around a secret. Doors multiplied without promise, and the women who moved between them drifted in their grey shifts like smoke denied a sky. Some murmured; some rocked; some stared at the windows as though the glass itself were a barrier between body and soul. I learned quickly to walk as they did, heel to toe, without question, until the nurses ceased to notice I was new.

They gave me a bed beneath a crucifix whose Christ had been bleached to ghostliness by years of scrubbing. The straw mattress was clean enough, the blanket thin enough to make gratitude feel like hypocrisy. Each morning a bell rang sharp as guilt, and we were marshalled into usefulness: needles for mending, brushes for scrubbing, hands for labouring over the same pale floor that never grew brighter. By afternoon we were granted small mercies such as paper scraps, broken pencils, a slate to cage our thoughts.

I wrote the same word again and again, as though repetition might form a ladder back to grace. Father. Father. Father. The chalk blurred where my fingers dampened it. The ward sister laughed and called me diligent. I did not tell her that I was performing a kind of prayer, no, a conjuring. A daughter's obedience written often enough might reach a heaven that had grown deaf. There were other names I could not write. One was a single syllable that had once belonged to a heartbeat. The chalk broke when I pressed too hard.

Time in Ravenbrooke had two measures only, waking and sleeping, and both too long. I learned its private music, three o'clock, when the vents exhaled their fat-smelling breath; four, when the crows came to the soot-black sill and tapped for entry; five, when the boiler wheezed like an old man remembering laughter. At six the warder passed with his keys whispering to each other. At seven the chaplain read a psalm, his voice carved clean of pity, and when he finished the ward lay beneath his Amen like a shroud.

It was on the fifth day or perhaps the sixth, for days there bred and devoured each other, that he came. I felt it first as a hush, the particular quiet that enters a room before authority does. He stood at the foot of my bed, just as he had once stood in the pulpit: hands clasped behind him, chin lifted, spine stiff with doctrine. The black of his coat swallowed light.

"You have been provided for," he said. His tone was ledger-like, an account closed. "You will remain until you have repented."

The voice I heard answer him was my own, yet thin and strange, as though borrowed from another bed. "I wanted only to be loved."

He looked at the crucifix, not at me. "Want is not virtue. You have brought disgrace upon your mother and upon me, and through us upon the Lord's house. Repentance is your portion now." He paused, then added, almost as charity, "Prayer will avail you if you do not flatter yourself with worldly hopes."

The nurses lingered in the doorway, admiring the performance of paternal duty. I pushed myself upright. "Forgive me," I said. "Only say it once."

He closed his eyes as though to bless me but no benediction came. When he spoke again it was with the stillness of judgment. "The wages of sin is death," he recited, "but the gift of God is eternal life." The words struck like iron dropped onto stone. He did not touch me. He bowed to the ward sister and turned away, his measured steps receding down the corridor just as they once had across our garden path on Sundays, when the Sabbath still smelled of lavender and not disinfectant.

That night I wrote the name until the chalk crumbled. The dust clung to my fingertips. I rubbed it into my skin until the word bloomed faintly there: Father. When the slate was taken, I had nothing left but the crucifix above me and the tick of the clock, a sound that ground the seconds like teeth. Night thickened. Some women moaned while one sang a lullaby that ended mid-note when her door was locked and another begged for water from a throat too dry to receive it. I counted the cracks in the ceiling until numbers became prayers. My hands folded of their own accord and would not be still. The skin at my wrists twitched with a thought that felt less like madness than command.

There was a nail loose at the base of the bed. I had noticed it from the first night, the way one notices pain one cannot name. When the ward slept its deepest sleep, the hour when even the keys seemed to dream, I worked the nail free. It came loose with a small sigh, as though grateful to serve. I raised my left wrist and pressed the point to where the veins ran blue and close to the surface. The first attempt faltered but the second found its purpose. I carved a cross no larger than a coin. The skin parted meekly. The pain was honest, simpler than the other kind, the invisible ache that had made a stranger of my own heart.

"He shall know my devotion," I whispered. Blood gathered in my palm like a small, bright chapel. I brought it to my lips, tasting iron and the sacrament of my own making. The ward did not stir. The

crucifix gleamed faintly, indifferent. I slept with my hand cupped over the mark so the sign would not fade back to flesh.

In the morning, they scolded and bound it. The doctor wrote something on his chart that was neither cure nor comfort, just a word that meant containment. They took the nail and left the smell of carbolic to do the rest. I lay still and obedient, tracing the cross on the inside of my eyelids until I could see it even with my eyes open. When the bell rang for work, the women filed out but I remained, and the crucifix remained, and the smell of soap hung over everything like false snow.

If the name on my palm was answered that day, I did not hear it. Yet sometimes, when the house is silent and the moon has thinned to a blade, the echo stirs in the wrist that remembers. The air thickens; the old scent rises from nowhere; and my lips move of their own accord. The prayer that comes is not the chaplain's. Hush now, little one. Hush.

10

The dawn broke over Branleigh Park in a silence too deep to be peaceful. The air was drained of colour; the sky hung pale as unwashed linen. Even the birds seemed uncertain, their tentative song trembling against a world not yet sure it deserved to wake. Mist rose from the ornamental lake, a veil of silver that blurred water, land, and reflection into one shifting surface. It was there, at the edge of the reeds, that the gardener found her.

Annie Larkin floated close to the bank, her pale hair drifting like weeds in the slow current, her skirts breathing faintly with the motion of the lake. Around her fingers wound the wooden rosary, the beads swollen and dark from the water, the crucifix glinting like something rescued and ruined all at once. Her face, half turned toward the sun's first light, bore no pain, or peace, only the stunned expression of one who has reached the end of her suffering without quite believing it.

When the alarm spread through the house, the mist was already thinning. Servants rushed along the gravel paths, their shouts thin as birdsong. Within the hour, the household stood gathered at the lakeside with Lord and Lady Spencer, the

Dowager, and Miss Marchwood among them, all pale, their hurried attire clashing with the soft brightness of dawn.

Georgina pressed a handkerchief to her mouth. "Oh dear heaven," she whispered. "How could this have happened?"

The gardener, hat crushed between nervous fingers, stammered that he had gone to skim the lilies, seen something pale beneath the water, and thought it a fallen gown.

"She was melancholy," Georgina said quickly, the lie shaped as kindness. "You remember, Mama, how she wandered alone at dusk. Perhaps she slipped whilst praying, maybe. It must have been an accident."

Charles nodded too readily. "Yes, of course. Poor creature."

But Beatrice's eyes stayed on the drowned form as the men lifted it from the reeds. "No," she said softly. "She was not one to surrender easily."

No one replied. The servants crossed themselves. The sky grew brighter, the light glancing off the lake until it seemed to burn.

Florence stood a little apart, the baby in her arms. Her expression was gentle, composed and so perfectly sorrowful that it verged on beautiful. "Poor girl," she murmured. "The Lord gathers those too gentle for this world."

Georgina seized on the comfort. "Yes," she breathed. "Perhaps that is true."

But Beatrice, leaning on her cane, watched her steadily. There was something rehearsed in the symmetry of her sorrow, something too exact to be grief. She opened her mouth to speak, then thought better of it.

By midday, the body was taken to the undertaker's in the village. Branleigh fell silent, the kind of silence that doesn't comfort but accuses. Clocks ticked faintly, as if wary of their own noise. Georgina shut herself in her room, saying she could not bear to hear a child's cry.

As dusk gathered, Florence sat alone in her chamber, the curtains drawn, the air thick with the smell of smoke and wool. On the table before her lay a small, worn prayer book, its gilt rubbed away, the name *Annie Larkin* written in a shy, cramped hand. She studied it a long while before striking a match. The candle flame trembled and then the paper caught. The gilt edges blackened, curled, and flared to life.

Florence watched without blinking as fire consumed the pages, word by word. The smoke rose in thin curls, the ghost of a prayer turning to ash. Her face, lit by the small flame, was tranquil, almost radiant. The reflection of fire glimmered in her eyes like recognition. She whispered something too low to catch and dropped the burning book into a basin. Ash scattered, faint and fragrant.

Outside, a wind rose, rippling the lake. The reflection of the house wavered, its windows blinking like uneasy eyes. In the nursery above, the baby stirred, whimpered once, and slept again. From her room, Florence smiled faintly, her hand tracing the air as though soothing something unseen. The candle flickered and went out, leaving behind the faint scent of smoke, an omen of a blaze still waiting to be born.

The morning of Annie Larkin's burial brought rain, not fierce, but steady and unending. It soaked through fabric, skin, and resolve. The churchyard lay grey beneath the low Buckinghamshire sky, the graves glistening with water. Annie had been given a pauper's corner, unadorned, humble, already sinking into mud. The servants of Branleigh Park came in black, their umbrellas bowed beneath the drizzle. The vicar's voice rose thinly through the rain, drained of conviction by repetition. When the final prayer was offered, the earth fell in slow handfuls, each sound heavier than the one before.

Florence stood apart, holding a small bouquet of lilies and rosemary. She waited until the last clod of earth fell, then stepped forward, placing her flowers with careful grace. Her lashes glittered with rain, though she did not shiver. Beatrice, watching from her carriage, saw the governess's lips move but some innate sense told her the words were not from Scripture. The thought chilled her even before the sound was lost to wind.

When the mourners departed, Florence lingered. She gazed at the mound, tilted her head as if listening, and whispered, "The Lord takes the weak first." Then she turned away, serene, and walked back through the rain.

That evening Beatrice spoke of it to Georgina as they sat in the drawing room. The fire burned low; rain traced the windows like tears.

"She said something at the graveside," Beatrice murmured. "I couldn't quite hear but I am sure it was, *The Lord takes the weak first.*"

Georgina, pale with fatigue, looked up from her embroidery. "It was only a sentiment, Mama. Miss Marchwood has a melancholy imagination. You yourself admit she is sensitive."

"Sensitive?" Beatrice repeated softly. "No. That isn't the word I would use any longer."

Georgina bent again to her stitches, unwilling to quarrel. "Let us not dwell. The house has had enough sorrow."

Beatrice said nothing more, but her gaze drifted to the dark window, where her own reflection watched her back.

In the days that followed, Branleigh's air grew heavy again. The nursery, once bright with play and chatter, turned still. The quiet there was not peace but presence. Servants passed the door softly, unwilling to look inside. At night, Hattie began to cry out in her sleep. Georgina came running to find her trembling, her voice small and certain.

"The lady from the lake came, Mama," she whispered. "She wanted to take my baby brother. I told her no."

Georgina's arms tightened around her child. "Hush, darling. It was a dream."

But even as she said it, she turned toward the doorway, toward a shadow that was not there.

Moments later Florence entered, candle in hand, her expression the picture of calm. "Poor little one," she murmured. "storm unsettles children." She took Hattie gently into her arms, and at once the child quieted, her sobs softening to hiccups.

"There now," Florence whispered. "Sleep beneath the roses, child. Sleep and fear no more."

The lullaby was low, mournful, and impossibly sweet. Georgina stood listening, uneasy, sure she had never heard the tune before. When the child's breathing steadied, Florence laid her down and brushed her hair from her forehead with a tenderness that seemed to mock its own perfection.

Downstairs, in the warmth of the kitchen, the servants whispered over the last of the tea.

"It isn't right," the cook said, crossing herself. "She's too calm. There's darkness behind her eyes, I've seen it."

The scullery maid nodded. "When she looks at you, it's like she's reading your sins."

"Mind yourselves," the butler warned, glancing toward the ceiling. "Walls carry words."

Above them, the lullaby began again, winding through the rafters, soft, measured, as lovely as it was wrong.

By morning, the rain had passed, but the house did not breathe easier. The air smelled faintly of damp earth and ashes. Somewhere in the distance, the chapel bell tolled once, slow, hollow, as though marking a death not yet named.

And in her room, Florence Marchwood awoke smiling.

. . .

The departure came without ceremony. Before the house had properly woken, Lord Charles's carriage rolled down the long drive toward London, the rhythm of its wheels beating like relief disguised as retreat. He had kissed Georgina's cheek lightly, murmured promises to return before the week's end, and gone without noticing that she had not replied.

His absence left the house breathing differently in an uneasy quiet that felt like reprieve and burden both. The silence that followed him was not peace but pause, as though Branleigh itself were listening for something. Beatrice had taken to her bed again, her strength faltering with each day. Georgina spent her mornings at the Dowager's bedside, her afternoons attending correspondence and household accounts, while the nursery slipped steadily into Miss Marchwood's keeping.

At first, it seemed an answer to prayer. Florence governed the children's world with faultless grace. Meals arrived punctually; tempers were soothed before they could spark. The nursery gleamed. Yet, beneath that order, something shifted. The rhythm of the house no longer belonged to Georgina and instead it pulsed to the governess's quiet design.

She noticed it first in the smallest ways: lesson books reordered, curtains drawn at unfamiliar hours, the air faintly scented with lavender not her own. When young Alice, the nursery maid, was dismissed to the laundry without notice, Georgina asked for explanation.

"The girl dropped the baby's bottle," Florence said gently. "It seemed prudent to relieve her of nursery duty for the child's safety. She is incompetent."

There was no fault in the reasoning, no hint of impertinence. Yet the steadiness in her tone, the calm certainty made Georgina's throat tighten.

That night, as she helped Beatrice sip her broth, she spoke of it. "She changes things without asking," Georgina said softly.

"Nothing overt, but the order feels... different. As though she is exerting a power or testing to see how far it can go."

Beatrice leaned back against her pillows, half-smiling, half-exhausted. "You must not fret over trifles, my dear. If she brings calm to the nursery, be grateful. The house needs a steady hand. But at the same time it will serve you well to be vigilant and maintain control of your home and children."

Georgina nodded, unease building beneath her composure. There was something about Florence's presence that seemed to linger after she had left a room, a sweetness that clung, faint as perfume, impossible to dispel and even at the mention of her name, it invaded once again.

Later, she climbed the stairs to bid the children goodnight. The nursery door stood ajar. Through it she saw Florence by the hearth, the baby cradled in one arm, Hattie leaning against her knee. Firelight burnished her face until it glowed like gold leaf, softening every edge into something saintly.

"Tell the end again," Hattie begged.

Florence smiled. "Just once more, then. *'And the lady took the child in her arms, and the storm was stilled, and the night was kind.'*"

Her voice wove through the room like silk. Georgina froze. The words were hers, the ending of a bedtime tale she had invented months before. Yet now it was another's mouth that gave them life, another's tone that carried their comfort.

When she entered, Florence rose at once, all grace and deference. "Forgive me, my lady. The children begged for their story, and you were occupied. I hope I have not presumed."

"Of course not," Georgina said, though her voice sounded thin, borrowed. "I thank you for your kindness."

She bent to kiss her daughter goodnight. But the child's eyes were already turned toward the governess with a gaze soft, worshipful, instinctive. It was a small betrayal, harmless perhaps, yet it struck Georgina with the precision of a pin.

That night, unable to pray or sleep, Georgina took some air. Mist drifted above the lawns, turning the garden to silver. The roses bowed like penitents. From somewhere high above, she thought she heard the faintest thread of song, a lullaby half-familiar, half-feared, winding through the dark.

In the nursery, Florence stood by her own window, the baby asleep against her shoulder, his breath warm on her collarbone. The candlelight carved her face into planes of gold and shadow. She gazed down toward the figure moving along the garden path below, Lady Georgina, black against the mist.

"She doesn't belong here anymore," Florence whispered.

The child stirred, and she bent to kiss his hair.

"Neither did I. And now, I do."

11

Winter at Ravenbrooke had a taste like iron on the tongue. The ward windows sweated with their own cold while frost wrote its white hieroglyphs across the panes and refused to melt, no matter how many buckets of hot water the nurses placed beneath them, as if steam might reason with December. I lay strapped to the bed after what they called an episode, a word far too small for what had happened. The leather bit at my wrists where the old cross-shaped scar slept beneath the skin, and the buckle at my waist pressed into bone with the slow insistence of a sermon

The lamps had been turned low with each flame trimmed to a stingy tuft. A draught ran along the floor like a stray animal searching for a crack in the wall. From the far end of the ward came footsteps, two sets, deliberate and unhurried. The doctor arrived wrapped in winter wool and the scent of carbolic, his nurse trailing close enough to catch his words before they faded. He did not look at my face first. He looked at the straps, then at the pulse in my throat, then at the crucifix above me, as though each were a gauge to be read before the soul it bound.

"Delusions of motherhood," he dictated. The nurse's pencil made

its neat obedience. "Persistent auditory hallucinations. Claims of hearing a child cry."

His English ticked like a metronome, his voice measuring the distance between sanity and convenience. I turned my head toward him though the collar allowed little movement. "I heard him," I said. The words left my mouth cracked and dry. "You were not there. I was."

He did not answer me. He named a powder and an hour and the nurse wrote both down as if recording a disease newly discovered. When her pen paused, it was not from pity, only from lack of flow. They left. The ward resumed its breathing with a cough that belonged to the timbers, the faint rattle of coal settling in its scuttle, a woman three beds down humming the fragment of a hymn that never found its ending. The straps cooled against my skin. I stared at the frost-filmed window and imagined stars behind the blur. If I named them, one for every letter of a name I dared not speak, perhaps the hours would move.

From the next bed came a whisper. The woman there was older than grief and thin as the seam of her own sheet. She never spoke by day. At night her voice slid through the dark like smoke under a door.

"You'll never get out of here, love. Once they've got you, they never let go."

Her certainty lay down beside me like a second blanket. I turned my head toward her voice, the strap rasping at my neck. "I shall leave when God opens the door," I said.

She made a sound that might have been laughter or mercy. "Then you'll wait forever." Her whisper thinned to silence, absorbed by the ward the way spilled water disappears into wood. I watched the weak lamp flame bow to its own breath, then steady again. I told my hands to be still. I told my wrists to believe in morning, even if I did not.

After a while, the corridor woke. Keys began their conversation,turn, withdraw, turn, withdraw, a litany of locks recited without words. The sound multiplied, echoing from one iron throat to the next until the whole building seemed to pulse with it. It was not sound but certainty: that every door in the world might close at once if a single will commanded it. The thought struck deep, a tolling beneath the ribs, and stayed.

The nurse came with the powder and the tepid water. I swallowed as instructed. The straps were loosed, not from kindness but efficiency. "Sleep now," she said, smoothing the blanket as though sealing a coffin. I turned my face to the thin pillow and above me, the pale Christ stared through everything. The draught at the floor found my ankles and held them in its cold hands until the medicine blurred the edges of the room and, for a heartbeat, made the air merciful. Far off, the keys turned again. The sound followed me downward, faithful as any psalm, and I knew as one knows a wound by its throb, that wherever I laid my head the doors would remember me. And close.

12

By late autumn, the trees along the drive stood half-bare, their branches black against a sky the colour of old pewter. Indoors, the air carried a damp chill, and the fires had to be coaxed constantly to life, as though the house itself resisted warmth. Once filled with children's laughter and servants' chatter, Branleigh now seemed to fold inward, breathing shallowly, as if conserving its strength.

Lady Beatrice Spencer seldom left her chamber. Her health had diminished quietly since Annie Larkin's death; her body, once unyielding, had begun to fail the discipline of her will. Georgina visited daily out of duty, but it was Miss Marchwood who came most often bearing trays and books of psalms, her calm presence settling like a benediction on the room.

At first, the visits were courtesy, then habit. By the third week, they had the structure of ritual. Each afternoon, when the rain began its faint, steady drumming and the lamps were lit, Florence entered the sickroom with her tray and a small, worn Bible. She would draw the curtains halfway but never fully, and sit at the dowager's side. Her voice, low and measured, filled the space with verses of mercy and trial, her tone gentle enough to make faith sound newly possible.

At first, Beatrice found comfort in the readings as the days were long and solitary. Florence's voice lent grace to the familiar and even her silences seemed shaped by reverence. But gradually, something shifted. The chosen psalms grew darker, the passages longer, the rhythm of her voice more deliberate. Gone were the soft assurances of rest and deliverance. Now she lingered on the psalms of vengeance, on words that spoke of wrath, and of the Lord's enemies brought low.

"Do you believe," Florence asked one afternoon, her gaze steady, "that God forgives all sins, my lady?"

Beatrice looked up from her tea. "I believe He forgives those who seek Him with humility."

"And what of those who were never offered mercy?" Florence turned toward the window, where the last of the ivy clung like a dying hand. "If the world condemns them first, what is left for God to forgive?"

Beatrice hesitated, unsettled by the intensity beneath the calm. "The world is cruel," she said at last. "But cruelty ends with The Lord. Faith teaches endurance."

Florence smiled faintly. "Endurance," she echoed. "Yes. Some are chosen to endure more than others."

Beatrice reached for her cup, startled by the tremor in her hand. "You speak like one who has suffered deeply, my dear."

Florence lowered her eyes. "We all have our share, my lady. Mine was more... thorough."

Something about the phrasing unsettled her listener more than any confession could have done. Beatrice felt a rush of pity that bordered on affection. "There's sorrow in your eyes, child. I pray it leaves you before it consumes you."

Florence's head lifted sharply, and for a heartbeat her

composure fractured. A fierce emotion, anguish, or something darker, flashed across her face before she rose, crossing the small distance between them. She took the dowager's frail hand in both of hers.

"You're kind to me," she whispered. "No one has ever been kind."

The pressure of her grip was startling, almost desperate. Beatrice felt the pulse beneath Florence's skin, rapid and ungoverned, fluttering like a trapped bird.

"There now, my dear," she said gently. "Whatever grief you carry, time will ease it. Peace always finds its way back."

Florence's breath caught. For a moment, Beatrice thought she might weep but the tears did not come. Instead, she released the older woman's hand, retreating a step as if ashamed. "Forgive me," she murmured. "The weather and close of winter sometimes makes me sentimental."

"Not sentimental," said Beatrice softly. "Only human."

Florence gave a fragile smile, curtseyed, and left. The door closed with its usual softness and Beatrice sat motionless, the imprint of those hands still tingling on her skin. She looked toward the window. Dusk had deepened; the glass reflected her own face or seemed to. For a moment she thought she saw another woman's shape layered over her reflection, upright and watchful, eyes gleaming faintly even in shadow. She blinked, and the image was gone.

"She is a poor, troubled creature," she whispered aloud, as if saying it might make it true. But the words did not sit easily in her mouth.

That night, as the wind moved through the eaves and the house groaned in its sleep, Beatrice lay awake. She thought of Florence's trembling hands, of the wild pulse she had felt, and the strange, yearning hunger in her eyes. It was not gratitude she had seen. It was need. Raw, ungoverned, and without end. And Beatrice, though she could not yet name the truth, knew in her bones that she had not comforted a lamb, but a wolf that had learned how to wear it's disguise well.

13

By November, Florence Marchwood had become the axis on which the household turned. Her calm, her voice, her insistence on order had reshaped every rhythm of the nursery until even the servants seemed to move in time with her. Hattie, once lively and wilful, was now subdued except in Florence's presence; she read only when Florence listened, obeyed only when Florence smiled. Baby Theodore, too, seemed bewitched and utterly docile in her arms, quiet at her touch.

To Georgina, it was as if her children had fallen under some wicked spell. Their obedience was not fear, nor respect, it was devotion, and it terrified her. One pale morning, the family gathered for breakfast. The light was thin, filtering through mist-fogged windows. Beatrice, fragile and withdrawn, toyed with her teacup while the servants moved softly around the table. Hattie sat beside her mother, humming under her breath. It was the lullaby.

"Sweetheart," Georgina said, forcing a smile, "have you finished your lessons for today?"

The child shook her head. "I'll wait for Mamma Florence."

The spoon slipped from Georgina's hand. It struck her plate with a sharp, shattering clang that froze the room.

"What did you say?"

Hattie's small face paled. "I... I meant Miss Florence," she whispered, shrinking back. "I didn't... "

Georgina rose, trembling. "You will never call her that again," she said, her voice breaking against the words. "Do you understand me? Never."

The child began to cry, small, frightened sobs that cut through the heavy air.

It was then that Florence appeared in the doorway. She paused just long enough to absorb the scene of the weeping child, the rigid mother, the servants frozen between duty and dread. Then she moved forward, her voice gentle, soothing, controlled.

"Dearest," she said softly, kneeling beside Hattie. "Come now, it's nothing. Mamma didn't mean to frighten you."

Georgina stiffened. Florence gathered the child into her arms, cradling her close, her cheek pressed to Hattie's damp face.

"There now, my darling. Hush. Mamma loves you very much. All is well."

It lasted only a minute, but the damage was done. When Hattie's sobs finally quieted, Georgina felt every gaze in the room upon her, including the servants' pity, Beatrice's silent disapproval of whom she wasn't sure, and Florence's gaze, serene and victorious.

"Thank you, Miss Marchwood," Georgina said coldly, reclaiming her composure by force. "You may take Hattie upstairs."

Florence rose, still holding the child. "Of course, my lady. She'll forget it all soon enough."

Their eyes met briefly. There was no humility in the

governess's gaze. Only calm, glittering certainty. When the door closed behind them, Georgina's strength dissolved. She sank into her chair, her breath uneven, her pulse fluttering at her throat. The room seemed to tilt. The murmured movements of the servants came and went like water, and she sat very still, staring at the trembling surface of her untouched tea and prayed for Beatrice to offer support or keep her counsel. The latter prevailed.

Later that evening, she stood outside the nursery door. The corridor was dark except for the line of lamplight spilling from beneath it. From within came Florence's voice, melodic, and unbearably tender.

Sleep beneath the roses, child,

Where no storm shall find you.

The tune drifted down the hall, slow and sweet as a sedative. Georgina pressed her palm to the wall, suddenly unsteady. The song felt older than the house itself, like something whispered to the dead. Something had to be done and she would speak to Charles the moment he returned.

That night, long after Branleigh had sunk into silence, Florence stood before her mirror. The candlelight played over her face, gilding it, softening it, turning her reflection into something both beautiful and strange. Behind her, the nursery slept and beneath them, something darker, like an insidious energy trapped beneath the floorboards. She lifted her hand to the mirror, fingertips grazing the glass. Her reflection seemed closer than her own skin, familiar, commanding, unyielding.

"You are almost mistress here now," she whispered.

The candle flickered. The words lingered, heavy, irrevocable.

14

The first frost had thickened across the lawns by the time Lord Charles returned to Branleigh Park. The gravel crunched beneath the carriage wheels, a sharp, deliberate rhythm that reached Georgina before the horses came into sight. From the parlour window she watched the dark shape of the coach draw near, her expression calm though her pulse quickened. He had been gone nearly a fortnight. His letters, few and perfunctory, had spoken of business in London but said nothing of when he would return, or whether he had wished to.

He entered with the air of a man who demanded welcome yet resented the need for it. His coat still carried the city's scent, smoke, rain, and filth and his boots bore the grime of distance. When Georgina stepped forward, his smile faltered almost before it formed.

"You look tired," she said.

"I am tired," he replied, his tone clipped. "The journey was intolerable. London's worse, with talk of plague and influenza."

"You might have written," she said quietly.

"I did write. Three times."

She lifted her chin. "Then the post must have failed, for I received none of them."

He gave a short, humourless laugh. "Careless, yes. That's the word for it. You must speak to the postmaster." He moved to the fire, holding his hands to the warmth. "I suppose you've had your governess for company in my absence."

Georgina flushed. "You wrong me, Charles. I have had no company but duty to this house, your mother's weakness, the children… "

"And what of you?" he interrupted. His weariness had sharpened into irritation. "You speak of duty as though affection were a sin. I come home to find the house colder than the weather. You've made it a tomb."

"Better a tomb," she said quietly, "than a house of whispers."

He turned, frowning. "Whispers?"

"About her," she said. "About Miss Marchwood. The servants gossip and even the villagers stare. Do you not see how they look at her? How they look at you? How rumours begin and wild imaginations run riot regardless of the facts or lack of them."

The words hung in the air like smoke, thin, choking, inescapable. Before he could reply, another voice entered the silence.

"Forgive me, my lord. My lady."

Florence stood in the doorway; a silver tray balanced in her hands. Steam curled from the teapot; the scent of bergamot threaded through the air. Her voice was soft, deferential, but there was intent in her timing, precision in her calm.

"I thought you might wish for tea after your journey," she said.

She crossed the room with measured grace, her steps scarcely disturbing the carpet. The lamplight caught the smoothness of her hair, the composure in her face.

Charles's expression softened. "That's thoughtful of you, Miss Marchwood."

"It is only my duty, my lord and the children are sleeping so I have moments to spare," she answered, pouring the tea with a steadiness that made the china seem to hold its breath. "We are all so glad you have returned safely."

Her tone was balm. The tautness in him eased; his shoulders dropped. "That is just what a weary man needs to hear," he said, half-smiling.

For a heartbeat, their eyes met, no longer than a breath, yet enough. The air shifted, charged and perilous.

Georgina's voice broke it. "That will be all, Miss Marchwood."

Florence inclined her head. "Yes, my lady."

She withdrew with her usual quietness, the rustle of her skirts receding like a sigh.

Charles watched the door close behind her. "You might have spared her that tone."

"I will not have her in here when we are at odds," Georgina replied.

"At odds," he repeated, the words curling in his mouth like smoke. "Yes. That seems to be our favourite state."

The quarrel that followed was brief but cutting with each phrase deliberate, each silence heavier than speech. By the time Charles left her standing by the fire, the room felt colder than it had when he first entered.

Upstairs, Beatrice Spencer had heard it all. She stood motionless on the landing, her hand resting on the banister. Below, she watched her son's figure pass through the hall with the same careless gait that had once belonged to his father. And behind him, a shadow glided almost unseen, the governess, head bowed, hands folded, her composure more dangerous than defiance. Beatrice closed her eyes. The ache that had been sleeping in her chest awoke with cruel familiarity.

It begins again, she thought.

The pattern repeated as it always had thanks to an indulgent man, a weary wife, and the serpent that slid, uninvited, between them.

Below, Florence paused at the foot of the staircase. For a moment, she thought she felt eyes upon her, but when she looked up, the landing was empty. Still, she smiled, small, secret, certain, and turned toward the nursery, *her* domain.

15

Night at Ravenbrooke was a thing that breathed. The wards exhaled rot and damp wool and drew in our fear as the pipes shuddered as if the building itself were sick with fever. Along the gallery, the lamps had been dimmed to a single one, a modest flame in a polished glass chimney, the ward's only moon. We slept as we always did in winter, beneath grey army blankets that smelled of sweat and death, on iron bedsteads bolted at the feet, the horsehair ticking prickling through if you turned too roughly. Somewhere, a woman prayed in a language I did not know. Somewhere, an attendant coughed, the keys at her belt giving a tired, metallic sigh.

The fire began with an act of ordinary disobedience. Mary, the one with the scar at her temple, rose before the bell and drifted toward the lamp, that small, forbidden sun. She was meant to be strapped at dusk, but the Matron had forbidden restraints except in violent cases, new rules from the Commissioners in Lunacy, so the leather wristlets lay unused in the drawer, smelling faintly of tallow. Mary reached out. The glass struck the corner of a Psalter left from the evening's reading, and the lamp toppled. The oil spilled like dark benediction across the boards. The flame followed, hungry and immediate, speaking a language every woman in that ward understood at once.

The first scream was a thread. The second pulled the whole cloth apart. Curtains made of serge caught, flared, and bloomed and the holland blinds became white fire. I sat up as the smoke found my throat and called for the night nurse. The ward key turned and failed. From somewhere above came the bell of the administration block giving three strokes, a pause, three more. The fire signal. I had heard it rehearsed in daylight, never believing it would find us by night. Now the air shook with the sound of running feet, men shouting from the porter's lodge, the rattle of the hose cart dragged from its shed. Doors slammed open, then closed, then stuck, as though the building itself could not choose between mercy and order.

Smoke pushed under the door, black as a sermon on damnation. A woman coughed until she spat red. I pulled my shift over my nose, tasted paraffin, and began the prayer the chaplain had given me in place of any comfort. Deliver me from bondage, O Lord. Deliver me. My hands found the latch with hands on the door that was meant to bolt from outside. It yielded, soft as a sigh, as if even the wood had grown weary of obedience.

The corridor beyond was a kiln. I dropped to my knees to find the cooler air along the floor. Through the haze I saw the scarlet seam of fire moving rapidly, a messenger announcing judgment. Matrons ran with their keys belling at their waists, shouting, "Unlock! Unlock!" in voices shrill with terror. A man swung the hose; the stream leapt and turned to steam before it touched the flame. The gas jets split, blue to yellow, hissing like serpents. A woman ran past me with her hair wrapped in a sheet, fell, and did not rise. I stepped over her because she was no longer a person, only part of the burning world I had to cross.

Memory fragments there. I recall the refractory room, its iron door glowing red along the edges; the airing-court gate flung wide by a porter whose hands shook so violently that his keys rang like rain; the day-room piano exhaling flame through its ribs until the hymn that once mocked us became intolerably loud inside my skull. Curtains collapsed into cinders that fell like black snow. My shift caught a spark and stitched itself with stars; I beat at them until the fabric smouldered into silence.

I ran, or thought I did, down the main gallery toward the airing court, past the visiting room where yesterday a wife had wept for a husband who would not take her home, past the dispensary where bottles burst from heat and made their own bitter weather. The fire bell would not stop. Men shouted for buckets and a warder sobbed, "My God, my God," like a boy failing his catechism. Doors opened that had never opened before. For once, at Ravenbrooke, the locks took pity on the living.

Outside, the night struck me full in the face with a slap of rain and cold air that tasted of salvation. The November drizzle hissed against the flames, making a vast whispering, as though the world itself had leaned close to hush the madness. Steam rose from the gravel; the lawns shone black as glass. I stood barefoot on the yard stones, the grit biting, the heat on my back like a hand urging me onward. For an instant the glare from the windows cast my shadow all the way to the boundary wall. Women poured into the court, some smouldering, some bleeding, some laughing as if the fire had burned away the need for sense. Attendants herded us toward the gate, then the road, anywhere that was not here.

I turned once. The asylum burned like revelation, the pavilions answering one another, the central tower a great candle that refused to die. The rain hissed; the carbolic turned sweet and foul in the steam. I pressed my palm to my wrist where the old cross lay beneath the skin, and said aloud, though none heard me, "I am free."

The road beyond the boundary was half mud, half frost. I walked into it barefoot, carrying nothing, because there was nothing left, no shawl, no book, no name that condemn me. The rain needled my scalp but the darkness did not care. Behind me, the bells rang themselves hoarse. Ahead lay only hedge after hedge, and a lane that learned the shape of my feet by heart before the night was done.

16

The morning after Charles's return broke pale and brittle, the frost lacquered the lawns and hedges until the whole of Branleigh Park seemed carved from glass. Florence Marchwood stood in the nursery, sorting the Hattie's lesson books, when a knock came at the door. The butler, deferential and precise, bowed slightly.

"His lordship wonders if you would join him for a turn in the gardens. Her ladyship is with Lady Beatrice and will not require you for the hour."

Florence hesitated only long enough to smooth her expression. "Of course," she said, and after donning her cloak, followed the path through the cold. Her breath rose in small ghosts before her as she walked. The rose garden waited in its slow ruin, blooms gone, beauty suspended on the edge of decay. Charles stood by the sundial, his coat unbuttoned, his face bright with the careless ease that had so often passed for charm.

"Miss Marchwood," he said, smiling. "I trust the children are well? It seems they flourish under your care."

"They are angels," she replied softly. "Children often are, before the world instructs them otherwise."

He laughed. "You speak as though you've lived a century. Come, let us walk. The rose bushes will not survive another frost, I fear."

They moved side by side down the gravel path, the frost crunching beneath their steps. The garden breathed its own slow death around them; the air was perfumed with cold earth and fading sweetness. For a moment, the silence between them felt almost companionable.

"You read, do you not?" Charles asked. "Georgina tells me you have a fondness for poetry."

"I do, my lord. But the Psalms are the truest verse. No poet writes of longing and temptation so plainly."

He smiled, amused. "Temptation, Miss Marchwood? A curious subject for a governess."

"Temptation is the test of the righteous," she said. Her tone was reverent, and without irony.

Charles chuckled lightly, turning his face to the thin sun. "Then righteousness must be the dullest virtue of all."

Her gaze lingered on him, steady, unblinking. He mistook the tremor in her hand for cold. At the far end of the garden, where the path curved toward an old marble bench, the rose bushes grew wild. The thorns clutched at the air like desperate hands. As Florence brushed past one, a thorn caught her finger. A small gasp escaped her; a drop of blood welled, bright as a garnet against the white of her skin.

"My dear Miss Marchwood," Charles exclaimed, catching her hand before she could withdraw it. "You must take more care."

"It is nothing," she murmured, though her pulse fluttered beneath his thumb.

He drew out a handkerchief of fine linen, his initials stitched in thread and wrapped it gently around her finger. "There," he said. "We cannot have our governess wounded in battle with the roses."

The fabric turned pink where her blood touched it. The intimacy of the gesture, a simple gallantry to him felt to her like sacrament. The garden seemed to tilt; even the light shifted, warm and perilous. She breathed in his nearness, the scent of tobacco and wool, the faintest trace of cologne. When he released her hand, she did not move at once.

"You are too kind," she said softly.

"Merely gallant," he answered with a laugh. "An old habit, I'm afraid."

They walked back toward the house in silence. At the terrace steps, she curtsied. "Good day, my lord."

"Good day." He turned away, already humming to himself.

Florence watched him go until the door closed behind him. The handkerchief still wrapped her finger; his scent clung to it. Later, in her room beneath the eaves, she unwound the linen, now stiff with her blood, and held it to her lips. Her eyes closed. The moment replayed, his voice, the heat of his hand, the ease of his smile. A shiver passed through her, exquisite and terrifying. She pressed the cloth harder to her mouth, then folded it carefully and placed it at the bottom of her trunk, beneath her Bible and the child's ribbon she always kept. For a long time she sat motionless, a faint smile touching her lips.

When Charles returned to the house, the first thing he did was pour himself brandy, too early an hour for civility, though he had never been troubled by civility. The fire in the library burned bright, throwing long arms of light across the room. He sank into his father's chair with the satisfaction of a man who believes he has escaped something, though from what, he could not have said.

He told himself that his walk with Miss Marchwood had been harmless and a courtesy extended to a devoted servant. Yet her words lingered: Temptation is the test of the righteous. It had unsettled him, not for what she meant, but for what he had felt. He smiled faintly, self-mocking. He had never been righteous, nor eager for the test.

Charles Spencer had been born to indulgence. His youth, Eton, then Oxford, was a procession of amusements and forgiven indiscretions. The world had always liked him: easy smile, graceful manners, the charm of a man who believed himself harmless. His father, Lord Henry Spencer, had been the same – gregarious, selfish, admired. Charles had inherited the model and mistook it for manhood. When the old man died, the title fit him poorly, as if tailored for a broader soul.

Marriage to Georgina had been prudent, arranged between families that valued lineage over temperament. She had been beautiful once, still was, though her beauty had cooled into restraint. Her affection came in careful measures, like medicine. Her composure made him feel examined, corrected. And when affection began to feel like obligation, he sought warmth elsewhere in harmless flirtations, small trespasses that soothed his vanity more than his heart.

Florence Marchwood had appeared at Branleigh like a benediction. Clever but modest, pious but not pious enough to irritate, she carried about her an aura of calm that he mistook for peace. Her admiration was quiet, uncalculated or so he believed. She listened with her eyes as well as her ears, and in them he saw something Georgina had long withheld, faith. Faith is the most intoxicating form of desire. He was not in love but he was remembered. Seen. Redeemed, for a moment, from mediocrity.

He thought again of the garden, of her blood bright against the frost. It had moved him strangely, as though something sacred had been offered and refused. The memory stirred a nostalgia he had no name for, perhaps the ache of youth, of potential, of being wanted simply because one existed.

He drained the glass and stood. Somewhere above, a door closed softly, Georgina, no doubt, but his mind did not climb toward her. It lingered among the roses trees, where frost and sunshine, decay or perfume in bloom blurred the line between beauty and betrayal.

"Temptation is the test of the righteous," she had said.

He smiled at his reflection in the window, though it looked older than he felt. "Then God must have an interest in me after all," he murmured.

Upstairs, beneath the eaves, Florence knelt before her trunk. She lifted the folded handkerchief and pressed it to her lips. The scent of him clung faintly to the cloth, mingling with the faint iron of her own blood. Her eyes closed.

He had touched her hand. That was all. And yet the touch had bound her more securely than a vow.

In Lady Beatrice's chamber the fire had dwindled to a dull glow, the embers pulsing faintly, stubborn as a dying heart. She sat at her escritoire, the circle of lamplight narrowing around her like a watchful eye. Before her, the paper waited, white, silent. Her hand trembled as she dipped the pen.

The house was subdued. Even the wind had stilled, its sigh caught in the eaves. From far below came the slow tick of the hall clock, the faint drag of coals being raked in the kitchen hearth. Beatrice had not slept soundly in many weeks because sleep had become a shallow tide, troubled by dreams that clung long after waking. But tonight it was not her dreams that disturbed her it was what moved beneath the surface of the waking world.

She began to write, her script fine and steady despite her trembling fingers.

October the 29th, 1884.

The governess frightens me.

The words sat stark and narrow upon the page, too sharp against the softness of the light. She stared at them until the ink shimmered slightly, as if the paper itself recoiled. Then, with a small breath, she continued.

There is something unnatural in her calm. It burns instead of soothes. Her piety is too fervent, her tenderness too exact. I have seen that brightness before, the light that belongs not to holiness but to guilt, and perhaps to madness. She believes herself chosen, I think. An instrument of God. And those who believe thus are rarely merciful.

A drop of ink fell, dark and round as blood. Beatrice blotted it, the motion hurried, her pulse climbing.

She thought of the governess's face that afternoon among the fading roses: the strange inward serenity, the eyes alight with a private revelation. Florence Marchwood was not wicked, no, not that, but there was a terrible purity in her, a moral fever that burned without smoke. Beatrice had known that kind of fervour once, in the pews of her late husband's church and a young woman who claimed she heard angels singing. The angels had turned on her in the end, their voices driving her to the river. Beatrice dipped her pen again, her hand slower now.

If strength allows, I shall write tomorrow to the agency in London that sent her. I must be sure of her character. It is my duty, for the children, if for no one else. Virtue can wear too fine a mask.

Her fingers cramped; the pen wavered. She forced one more line, thin and uneven.

Yet I am very weak, and the hour is late. Tomorrow, perhaps.

She set the pen down and pressed her fingertips to her temple. The lamplight trembled, gilding the ink like something alive. And then faint, unmistakable, a sound.

A voice, drifting upward from the servants' quarters. Soft, measured, sweet as something meant for a cradle.

Sleep beneath the roses, child.

Beatrice froze. The pen rolled from her hand, struck the desk, and lay still. The melody wound through the air, patient and unhurried, the voice low and sure. It was the same tune she had heard whispered through the corridors at night, the same that haunted her sleepless hours. She stood, every movement deliberate, and went to the door. The song rose and fell, punctuated by the small, rhythmic scrape of a needle drawn through cloth. The governess was awake, mending, humming as she worked. To others, it might have sounded gentle, domestic. To Beatrice, it was something else entirely, perhaps a promise, a summons, a lullaby for the living.

She lingered at the threshold, then returned to her desk. The words she had written stared back at her. *Tomorrow, perhaps.*

Her throat tightened. Tomorrow would not be soon enough. The lamp flickered, its flame bending in a sudden draught, then righting itself with quiet defiance. The fire in the grate gave one last sigh and sank into ash. And Beatrice felt something akin to dread flood her bones. Tomorrow, she would send the letter.

17

The night after the fire, I walk because there is nothing else to do. My feet have learned the shapes of stones. Every few steps a thorn remembers to claim its tithe from my heel, and I pay it, and go on. The smell is wet earth, soaked ash, and the faint iron sweetness of blood when the skin breaks on my soles.

The sky gives no light of its own. It is the colour of dirty wool and presses low enough to touch. A wind comes in sideways, sprinkling the hedgerow with tiny beads that find the threadbare places in my shift and make their way in. I drink from the road because the road offers. I go down on my knees and cup the water in my hands, and the puddle tastes of hoof but I still drink, because it is given without question, and that is grace enough for now.

Fields stretch wide to either side, heavy with stubble and the black tongues of rooks hunched in the oaks. Somewhere, a sheep calls and a dog answers without interest. When I stop, the sound that remains is the small, patient click of water falling from the hedge into the ditch, as if the night itself were counting. I count with it, breaths, steps, the distance between one mercy and the next. The road turns and turns again. A fingerpost looms at a bend, its paint flaked, its letters enduring: Thame one way, Aylesbury the other, Oxford farther still. I turn toward the word that sounds like deliverance and move as if language itself could carry me.

I pray aloud because silence has teeth. "Deliver me from bondage, O Lord." The wind takes the words and lays them in the ditch, and I say them again. I do not ask to be warm. I do not ask to be found. I ask only that the door that opened once should not close before I reach it.

Dusk thickens early when the year is dying. It does not fall, it curdles, like broth left too long on a weak flame. By the time I reach the crossroads the light has pooled low on the horizon in a final, sullen bruise. My feet no longer remember which way they meant to go. I am thinking of lying down, the ditch is not unkind if one keeps one's head above the mud and then I see it, a square of gold carved into the rain beyond the hawthorn hedge. Between me and the glow lies a gate that protests on one hinge, and a strip of yard churned to paste by cartwheels and hooves.

I press my palms to the wood and lean through the hedge's bitter green. There it stands, set a little back from the road: a coaching inn, its signboard creaking on a chain. The painted horse upon it gallops in perpetual daylight, though daylight lives only in the paint. A lantern hangs above the arch that leads to the stables; its light writes every nail-head in bright ink. From within comes laughter that strikes the rafters and falls again with the clatter of plates. The smell drifts out in waves, ale, hot fat, wet horse, and the clean, peppered breath of a fire innocent of fear.

My legs fold as though instructed. I sink to my knees beneath the window, the one that shows a corner of a settle, a man's sleeve, the swing of a maid's apron. The sill is warm through the rain, warmed by lamps and bodies and the good temper of food. I press my temple to its edge and listen the way the dead must listen when the living speak above them.

Voices gather and scatter. At first they are only sounds, coins, laughter, the scrape of chairs. Hooves stamp in the yard and a hosteler curses softly, and a horse answers through its nose. Then, clear as struck glass, a woman's voice rises. She is young, not a girl, not yet worn. I can tell by the way she asks and answers without apology. "I'm bound for Oxfordshire," she says to someone I cannot see. "The Spencer family, Branleigh Park. My coach takes me at first light."

There are three names the world has taught me to recognise: the county that means escape, the family that means shelter, the house that means belonging. I close my eyes. The rain threads my hair and runs to my mouth, tasting of dirt and God's endurance.

"He sends me where I am meant to go," I whisper, and the words settle inside me as if they have been waiting for the hollow I have carried since the night the locks forgot their duty and the doors opened of their own accord.

18

By December, the rhythm of life at Branleigh Park had changed so gradually that no one could say when the shift had begun. Frost came early that year, whitening the lawns until they glittered like salt beneath the low sun, and the trees stood stripped bare, their branches rattling faintly in the wind like bones. Indoors, fires burned from morning till night, but the warmth never seemed to reach the marrow of the house. Beneath its polished calm, something colder had taken root.

Florence Marchwood now moved at the centre of it all. Her footsteps set the day's rhythm and her voice threaded through every corridor. She was neither servant nor mistress, and yet the household bent to her as if drawn by some quiet gravity. At dawn, her tread sounded on the nursery stairs. Soon followed the hush of her teaching, the murmur of her hymns, the faint clink of the spoon she used to measure the infant's milk. Order had replaced ease and reverence had replaced laughter.

Even Georgina, once the house's undisputed keeper, felt the ground beneath her slipping. Hattie no longer sought her lap for comfort. Theodore, when he fussed, turned instinctively toward the governess's arms. Florence accepted these small surrenders with the same mild grace she showed in all things.

"The children find routine soothing, my lady," she said once, when Georgina's voice sharpened. "They know where they are safe."

It was said gently, almost kindly and yet Georgina heard in it the unmistakable sound of criticism and dismissal.

Charles, blind to the undercurrent, was grateful for the peace. His household, he told himself, had been restored. "You've brought calm to this place, Miss Marchwood," he said one morning in the library, offering her that half-playful smile he once reserved for his wife.

"My gratitude and Georgina's, I'm sure, belongs entirely to you."

"I serve as I can, my lord," Florence replied, lowering her gaze.

It was he who broke the final boundary. Georgina constantly pled fatigue, Beatrice was ailing, and dinner seemed dreary with only silence for company.

"Miss Marchwood," he said lightly, "you must dine with us this evening. It will save formality. You know the children's affairs better than anyone."

The servants froze at his words. A governess at the family table. Such a thing belonged to gossip, not practice. Florence hesitated, the picture of humility. "I would not presume… "

But Charles waved her concern away. "You've earned it."

That night, she entered the dining room in dove-grey silk, modest but immaculate. Beatrice sat pale and watchful, her shawl drawn tightly. Georgina, silent, looked carved from marble. Florence ate sparingly, spoke little, and yet commanded attention as surely as if the room itself deferred to her. Charles laughed too freely; Beatrice's hands trembled on her napkin.

Later, in the drawing room, Beatrice caught her son's arm.

“Charles,” she said, her voice low and urgent, “you are making a fool of yourself.”

He frowned. “Really, Mother. Your piety blinds you. The woman is a saint so why fear her?”

“She is something,” Beatrice murmured. “But saints seldom leave warmth in their wake.”

He laughed, dismissive, kissed her hand, and walked away. She watched him go, watched Florence’s candle glide past in the hall, its flame doubling in the gilt frames like a procession of ghosts.

That night, as the rest slept, Florence sat in her attic room beneath the eaves. The candle beside her guttered low, throwing its light over an open journal, the cheap blue kind kept by schoolgirls and penitents. Her writing was small and even, each line pressed deep into the page.

They think I serve them, but I serve only the Lord. He has placed me here with purpose. The proud shall be humbled, and the barren heart made fruitful. I am His vessel. I am His handmaid. And He wills that I be loved.

When she stopped, her face had the stillness of prayer. She closed the book, pressed it to her chest, and blew out the candle. From the next room came the thin cry of the waking child. Florence rose at once, moving through the dark as though guided by invisible light.

The nursery, once a place of bright disorder, had grown to perfection. Not a toy out of place, not a wrinkle in a coverlet. The neatness felt devotional, oppressive, as though childhood had been trained into obedience. Georgina noticed it only gradually. Then, one morning, entering without warning, she stopped short.

The portraits were gone. The miniatures that had once shown her family, her parents, her brother in uniform, her childhood home, had vanished from the walls. In their stead hung a series of delicate pencil sketches: a lamb in a field, a sleeping child, a bird on a branch. Lovely, but sterile.

"Where are the portraits?" Georgina demanded.

Florence turned, arranging the children's shoes near the hearth. "The little one found them frightening," she said gently. "She told me the faces looked cross."

"Cross?" Georgina echoed.

"Children's fancies," Florence said with a soft smile. "I thought to quiet her dreams."

"You had no right to alter this room," Georgina snapped.

Florence bowed her head. "Forgive me, my lady. I only meant to serve the child to my best ability."

The words were humble but the glance that followed was not. Later, alone, Florence smoothed the edges of her sketches and whispered, "The vanity of the parent should not trouble the innocent."

Downstairs, the day moved on with its brittle quiet. Beatrice, frail but still sharp-eyed, took tea in the morning room. Florence brought the mail, she was passing and it was no trouble, her voice steady as ever. When she left, the older woman sat in silence, listening to the muffled lullaby drifting down from above. Something in that melody with its measured sweetness made her skin crawl.

That afternoon she climbed the stairs. The nursery door stood ajar. Inside, the air was faintly perfumed with soap and ash. The washbasin by the window was half full of water, still and dark. Floating in it lay Hattie's finest doll, its muslin dress grey and heavy, its flaxen curls plastered to its painted skull. Needles pinned the hem so it would not rise.

Beatrice crossed the room and lifted the doll. Water streamed from its limp body, cold down her arm.

"Poor thing," said a voice behind her.

Florence stood in the doorway, calm, composed.

"I found this," Beatrice said.

"Hattie must have done it," the governess replied softly. "She baptises her toys sometimes. Children play such curious games."

"With pins in their dresses?"

Florence smiled faintly. "They imitate what they dream, my lady."

Beatrice's breath caught. "Some games, Miss Marchwood, are the Devil's work."

For a moment, Florence's expression did not change. Then she smiled again, so gentle, so radiant, with a river of cold running beneath.

"Only when they end badly."

The stillness that followed was unbearable. Beatrice set the doll down and turned away, her pulse wild beneath her lace collar. Behind her, Florence wrung out the doll's gown, water dripping to the floor like tears. She began to hum, the same soft, patient refrain that had haunted the house for weeks.

Sleep beneath the roses, child.

Outside, snow had begun to fall, thin, soundless, inexorable, covering the garden paths in white. Inside, Branleigh Park held its breath, preparing to be smothered, not by a blanket of snow, by something far more insidious.

Beatrice Spencer sat long after the encounter in the nursery, her hands folded upon the coverlet as though in prayer. The doll's drowned face would not leave her, the pale curve of its cheek, the deliberate cruelty of the pins. She told herself she was too old to be frightened by such trifles, yet fear has no respect for age. Once it enters a house, it stays. Once it finds a heart, it settles there.

The fire had burned low. Its glow carved slow, uncertain

shapes across the walls, light and shadow shifting in uneasy rhythm. In the mirror, her reflection flickered, a ghost of an old woman watching herself fade. The ache in her chest pulsed with each shallow breath. It was not pain that frightened her most but recognition and the sense that something unseen had taken possession of Branleigh's quiet halls, as if the walls themselves leaned closer to listen. Waiting. But for what?

She reached for her Bible, its pages soft and worn from decades of prayer, and tried to read. But the words blurred, sliding from the page as though unwilling to be summoned. Her thoughts, traitorous, turned instead to the governess. *The girl is devout,* she told herself. *Too devout, perhaps. But she means well. She must.*

Yet when she closed her eyes she saw Florence Marchwood's face and the pale calm of it, the smile that trembled on the edge of restraint, never quite touching her eyes. She remembered the grip of the girl's trembling hands weeks before, the rush of emotion so fierce it had frightened her. Gratitude, Florence had called it. Beatrice had answered with kindness, believing it harmless. But kindness, she now understood, can be abused. It invites entry. It invites trespass.

A knock came at the door. Beatrice's heart lurched before she caught herself. It was only Georgina, her shawl gathered close, her face drawn with sleeplessness.

"Mama," she said softly. "I thought you might want company."

Beatrice gestured to the chair near the fire. "Sit down, my dear. You look worn to the bone."

They sat together in silence. The fire crackled faintly; the wind pressed and sighed at the window. When Beatrice finally spoke, her voice was low. "Tell me, Georgina, does the governess still trouble you?"

Georgina hesitated. "Trouble me, how?"

"Her influence grows too strong," Beatrice said. "Over the children. Over your husband. And over this house. I see it plainly, though others will not."

For a long moment Georgina said nothing. Then, in a voice small with weariness, "Charles insists she is a blessing, Mama. He says I should be grateful and I am so weary all of the time I do not have the energy to fight him."

Beatrice gave a bitter smile. "Men have always mistaken silence for virtue. Your father-in-law was the same. It pleased him to be tempted by women who prayed as they sinned."

Georgina's gaze sank to the fire. "Do you think she means harm?"

Beatrice paused, the question hovering like smoke between them. She wanted to say no, to dismiss it as an old woman's fancy. But truth has a way of forcing itself through frail lips. "I think she believes herself chosen," she said at last. "And those who are certain they serve Heaven are often the quickest to play God."

Her strength faltered; she leaned back, her breath shallow. "I mean to write to the agency in London. Her references, her past, must be known. It was foolish to delay."

"You're not well enough," Georgina said gently.

"Then you must do it for me, find the strength" Beatrice whispered. "Before it's too late. We have been too forgiving, dearest one and now we must act."

Georgina hesitated, then nodded. "I will. I promise."

When her daughter had gone, Beatrice sat motionless, listening to the long sigh of the house settling into its nocturnal stillness. The great clock struck ten, each chime fainter than the last. Then, from somewhere above, it came, the tune she had learned to dread.

Sleep beneath the roses, child.

The sound drifted down through the floorboards, so soft and

measured that it might have been a prayer. It threaded itself through the silence, winding around her thoughts until even her heartbeat seemed to follow its rhythm.

She pressed a trembling hand to her chest. "Lord preserve us," she whispered. "There is something unholy here."

Her eyes fell upon the pen and paper lying ready on the escritoire. She tried to rise, to set down her warning, but her limbs had grown too heavy. The last coal in the fire turned to ash. Still the lullaby went on, slow and unending, as though meant to soothe the living into surrender yet in reality it was a form of torment.

When sleep at last claimed her, it was not gentle. She dreamed of Branleigh Park alight, its windows blazing like the eyes of some vast creature feeding on its own heart. Flames climbed the nursery walls, and over the roar she heard the governess's voice, calm and sure, whispering:

It is the Lord's work.

And when Beatrice woke, the sound still echoed in her chest like a second heartbeat, steady, relentless, and not her own.

19

Winter had fastened its grip on Oxfordshire. The countryside lay entombed beneath snow and silence, the air so still that even the crows seemed to have forgotten their own voices. Roads vanished into drifts; the village church bells went unheard; and Branleigh Park stood alone within a white, muffled world. Inside, fires blazed from dawn until dusk, but the warmth did little to comfort. It did not soothe a house almost possessed.

The nursery had become Florence Marchwood's dominion. Day and night, her presence filled it, the steady rustle of her skirts, the low murmur of her songs, the soft tread of her feet between cradle and chair. Her voice was the first sound the children heard each morning and the last before sleep. Hattie sat at her lessons quiet as a shadow, her once-bright chatter worn down to docility. But it was Theodore who had become the true object of Florence's devotion, the small, beating centre of her private faith.

He was seldom out of her arms. The nursemaid's usefulness had dwindled to nothing and Georgina's motherhood had been reduced to ceremony. When she tried to take her son, the child shrieked in a way that felt almost unnatural, like a creature torn from its host.

One bleak morning, desperate to reassert her place, Georgina waited until Florence bent to tend the fire. “Let me take him,” she said lightly, holding out her hands. “He should remember his mother’s arms.”

Florence turned, her expression serene. “Of course, my lady.” She passed the baby across, gentle as a priest offering communion.

The change was instant. Theodore stiffened, his face darkened with panic, and he began to wail, an unearthly cry that pierced the air.

“Shh, my darling,” Georgina whispered, rocking him. “It’s only Mama.”

The screams grew worse. The child kicked and thrashed, his tiny fists striking her chest. Florence stood a few paces away, her hands folded neatly at her waist, her eyes bright with a strange, tranquil pity.

“He is tired, my lady,” she said softly. “He knows my touch. Allow me to calm him.”

But Georgina clutched him tighter. “He must learn me again,” she said through her teeth. “He is mine.”

The baby’s cries swelled until they filled the room, shaking the windowpanes. At last Georgina faltered. “Take him, then,” she snapped, her voice cracking.

The moment the child returned to Florence’s arms, the crying stopped. He nestled against her chest, his small hand curling into the fabric at her collar. Florence rocked him, her voice low and certain. “There now. No harm has come to you. I am here little one.”

The words were tender, but they rang like an oath. Georgina turned away, her knuckles white on the back of a chair. “You spoil him,” she whispered.

Florence smiled faintly, eyes lowered to the sleeping child. "He needs only love, my lady. The world offers too little of it."

From that day, the boy refused all others. Even the servants whispered that the child had been claimed, that he knew only her scent, her hands, her lullaby.

Each afternoon, Florence sat by the nursery window, the baby pressed to her shoulder. Outside, snow drifted endlessly, soft as ash. Inside, the fire burned steady and gold. She rocked, her lips near the child's ear.

"You are my flesh," she murmured, "my redemption."

She did not hear the door open. Beatrice Spencer stood on the threshold, having heard the words, breath catching in her chest. The sight before her, the governess caught in reverence over the sleeping child might have passed for sanctity, but every fibre of Beatrice's failing body recoiled. The air in the room was too close, the stillness too deep. Devotion, she thought, should never look so much like possession.

When Florence looked up at last, her composure was unbroken. "My lady," she said softly. "Forgive me. I did not hear you enter."

Beatrice gripped her cane, her breath thin. "You are devoted beyond measure, Miss Marchwood. The boy is fortunate to be so loved."

Florence's eyes gleamed. "Love is duty, my lady. I seek only to protect the innocent."

Beatrice studied her face. "Love that binds or possesses is not love," she said slowly. "It is hunger in disguise."

Florence smiled, a small, radiant thing that did not reach her eyes. "Then perhaps my love is of another kind."

Outside, the snow thickened against the windows, muting the light. Beatrice turned away, her heart labouring with the certainty that something within Branleigh Park had begun to decay from the inside out. She walked the corridor slowly, each step echoing like a question the house itself refused to answer. Behind her, the fire in the nursery burned low. Florence bent over the child once more, her lips brushing his hair.

"Hush now," she breathed. "You are safe with me. No one will ever take you from me."

Beatrice gasped, knowing that the governess had stepped over a line, had become brazen, almost fearless. Her words were a prayer, a vow, and a curse spoken in one breath.

20

Although the night had been long, plagued by restlessness and when it graced her, tortured sleep, Lady Beatrice Spencer had never been a fanciful woman. A lifetime of discipline had burned the sentiment out of her, and illness had taught her to mistrust imagination. Yet lately she lived in a kind of waking dread, quiet, constant, and formless. It was not death she feared. It was the governess.

The signs were small, almost delicate. Miss Marchwood's composure too steady to be natural and there was the strange gleam in her eyes when she looked at the infant and the faint murmur of her voice in the hall long after others had gone to bed. And always that serenity, unbroken, absolute, inhuman.

There was no cause for dismissal. No insolence, no impropriety, nothing that could be named. And yet Beatrice knew that such perfection was never the work of God.

That afternoon, as snow beat softly against the windows, she sent for Mrs. Dobbs, the housekeeper, a stout, no-nonsense woman whose loyalty had survived two generations of Spencer tempers.

"Mrs. Dobbs," Beatrice began, her tone low but steady, "you

recall that Miss Marchwood came to us through a London registry?"

"Yes, my lady. Gresham's Select Registry. The letter was very proper, on fine paper, in an elegant hand."

"Do you still have it?"

Mrs. Dobbs frowned. "It'll be in the servant file, my lady. Shall I fetch it?"

"Do so," Beatrice said. "Now, if you will."

When the woman returned, she bore the folded letter on a tray as though it were a relic. Beatrice adjusted her spectacles and read. The paper was expensive, the seal broken, the handwriting graceful. Everything appeared correct, until she came upon one small line.

The applicant bears a slight limp, the result of a childhood riding accident.

Beatrice frowned. In all the months Florence Marchwood had moved through Branleigh's corridors, she had never once faltered. Her step was soundless, fluid, unnervingly graceful.

"Mrs. Dobbs," Beatrice said, tapping the page with a trembling finger, "have you ever noticed the governess favour one leg?"

The housekeeper shook her head. "No, my lady. She walks as straight as a reed and chases Mistress Hattie like a whippet."

Beatrice's mouth thinned. "Then perhaps her lameness, like her humility, is of the useful variety."

She dismissed the housekeeper and sat for a long time staring at the snow beyond the window, the letter heavy in her lap. At last she dipped her pen and began to write, each word slow, deliberate, the ink trembling with her pulse.

To the Proprietress,

Gresham's Select Registry for Governesses, London.

. . .

Madam,

I write concerning Miss Florence Marchwood, lately in your recommendation. Certain irregularities compel me to request further particulars regarding her background, health, and prior situation. I ask that you treat this inquiry in confidence and respond with haste.

Yours faithfully,

Dowager Beatrice Spencer, Lady of Branleigh Park.

When she finished, she sealed the envelope with her signet and called for her maid.

"Clara, see this is placed with the post in the morning. It is private. Tell no one and keep it safe until then."

The effort left her drained and she asked Clara to help her to be where she slept fitfully, dreaming of footsteps in the hall.

Sometime near midnight, those footsteps came. Florence Marchwood moved through the corridors with her usual noiseless grace, candlelight shivering across her face. Passing the dowager's private parlour, she saw the flicker of a lamp and paused. After a moment, she knocked softly. When there was no answer, she slipped inside.

Clara was there, bent over the escritoire, sorting papers. She started when the governess appeared.

"Oh, Miss Marchwood, you frightened me!"

Florence smiled, sweet and low. "Forgive me. I saw the light and feared her ladyship might need assistance. You're diligent to watch so late."

Clara blushed. "She asked me to tidy her correspondence."

Florence's gaze drifted to the desk. Among the neat piles of paper lay a single envelope, sealed in red wax, set apart from the rest. "So conscientious," she murmured. "I do hope everything's properly closed, her ladyship hates a draft in the mornings."

"Everything's quite secure and I am aware of her ladyships preferences," Clara said quickly.

"Then let me help you," Florence replied, stepping closer. "You must be weary. Go and rest. I'll finish here."

The girl hesitated, flushed red and then obeyed. When the door closed, silence returned. Florence stood motionless a moment, the candlelight catching the faint rise and fall of her breath. Her eyes fell to the envelope. Her fingers brushed it lightly, tracing the seal. The wax gave way beneath her thumb with the gentlest pressure. Her eyes moved swiftly over the page. Then again, slower. When she smiled, it was with a quiet understanding that seemed older than she was. The letter touched the flame of the lamp. For a second, the handwriting flared gold, then blackened and curled to ash.

By morning, the post went out as usual. The letter was there but inside, a blank piece of paper that would no doubt cause the recipient a moment of curiosity. But the truth of it had already risen in smoke through the chimney, carried into the white sky.

Beatrice said nothing at breakfast and instead imagined her letter making its way to London. Her face was colourless and her hands were unsteady as she stirred her tea. Only her eyes betrayed her, the fierce, lucid certainty that had once made her formidable.

Later, alone in her chamber, she sat staring at the dying fire. The house was silent, muffled in snow. Yet somewhere above her head she thought she heard a voice, faint and melodious, humming the lullaby that had begun to haunt her sleep.

Sleep beneath the roses, child. While I watch over you. Seeing all, seeing all.

She closed her eyes. The sound and the words, new and meaningful seemed to seep into the walls.

Is she trying to tell me something, taunting me? Beatrice asked herself. *She knows. She has found me out. But how?*

The realisation struck with the slow inevitability of winter settling upon the land.

Outside, snow thickened, erasing footprints, swallowing paths. Inside, the Dowager felt the chill enter her bones, not from age, but from the knowledge that the house was home to one with a stronger will than her own. She was cunning and malevolent and Beatrice was suddenly afraid.

21

The inn breathes as a body does, drawing in smoke and ale and laughter, then exhales steam to the yard where the horses stamp and shake their tack. I crouch beneath the window, my toes sunk in the churned November mud, the hedge dripping on my neck. The pane is unlatched and pushed up a crack for air and its sash rattles faintly when the door within opens and shuts. I am close enough to smell the stew and the damp wool of travellers' coats, close enough that the candle's heat warms the sill against my cheek.

"You'll do well there," says the innkeeper's wife, a broad voice with flour on it. "A grand place, Branleigh Park. The Spencer's are gentry proper."

"I hope so, ma'am," says the other voice, the one that stops the air in my throat. She stands on the threshold between one obedience and another and is pleased to be standing there. "I have never been so far from Cheltenham. The agency speaks well of the family. I am to go at dawn. I shall be caring for a girl and a baby boy."

She laughs then, soft, careless, the sort of laugh that trusts the next hour to keep its promises. The floorboards creak. A cup is set down. I let my eyes close because the world behind the lids is steadier than the one outside them. The names the woman makes with her mouth strike me like flints. Oxfordshire. Branleigh Park. Dawn. Girl. Baby boy. Baby boy, baby boy. My heart begins to pound.

Later, when the house grows sleepy and the last plates clatter back into their places, I slip round to the yard where the carts are kept and stand beneath the jut of the window. The lantern over the arch throws a puddle of light that stops just short of the hedge. I put my hands to the sill, one, then the other and find the place where the paint has worn away under years of elbows and damp weather. The sash lifts without argument. I climb.

Inside, the air is thick with the day's use, soap, damp linen, the shadow of mutton and beer. The candle hisses and steadies. She is asleep already, turned on her side, her hair spread like dark corn-silk over the pillow's edge. The innkeeper's wife has set a tray with a heel of bread and cheese on the table and a small ewer by the washstand. On the chair lies a grey travelling gown, brushed and folded, and a bonnet with its ribbons tied neatly into a bow which tells me much of the wearers personality.

I sit on the edge of the bed, light enough that the mattress does not complain, and touch her hair with my fingertips. It is fine, warm still from the day, and my hand, one that has known straps and stone and the stink of burned serge remembers how to be gentle. She stirs and does not wake. I bend until I can smell her neck where it meets the pillow, a clean smell, untroubled. "It should have been me," I whisper, and the words do not sound like accusation, only like a fact the air has been waiting to hear.

I take the pillow in both hands and lower it to her face as a mother might lower a blanket to a child's chin. She wakes into the darkness I have made for her, and for a heartbeat her breath takes mine with it and then the room knows only the shared labour of her struggle and my decision. The body learns quickly what the mind refuses. This is a prayer, and prayers are acts done with the whole of a person. My arms hold steady. Her heels beat once against the mattress, twice, her hands find my wrists and slide away. It does not take long. When it is over, the silence returns as obediently as a servant called back to the door. I lift the pillow and place it gently where it lay before. The candle shows me a face emptied of its future, and I think, She looks asleep. I smooth her hair where my hand has mussed it, because it is a discourtesy to leave a woman untidy.

After, the room is very clear to me, as clear as a ledger. I dress her in my worn and filthy shift and take her gown for myself, one sleeve catching where the seam is narrow at the shoulder. Her boots fit if I do not mind the pinch. I tie the ribbons of her bonnet under my chin, and it shadows the fever that still lives in my eyes. In the looking glass over the washstand, the woman who looks back has composed herself; she is no longer a patient or a penitent. She is a governess with a journey at dawn. I remove the bonnet and look forward to wearing it again soon.

I focus on the task in hand which will forge the route to a new life. There is a way to lift a weight that has been a woman without disrespect and I find it. The yard below is dark and smells of horse and damp straw. I lower her out of the window and hear the thud as she lands, then I follow, my hands remembering the sill as if they had been taught the lesson in a gentler school. The hedge weeps on my neck again. Beyond the yard, the copse begins, a tangle of hawthorn and ash that will keep a confidence if asked properly.

The snow has not come yet but the ground is slick with the last of autumn. I drag her into the trees, feet first, her heels cutting little furrows where the leaf-mould is thin. I take her as far as I must to be out of sight of the yard and set her down beneath a stand of holly where the berries look like small, watchful eyes. My hands ache. Then I search with my foot until I find a stone that fits the palm well and sits heavy there without promising to jump. It is best if the world cannot recognise what it has lost. I kneel and do what remains to be done. The sound is the sound stones make when they are asked to finish a sentence. Leaves shift. An owl moves once and resettles itself on its private throne. When I am finished, the face no longer holds a future anyone can claim. It is a mercy of a kind. It is also a wall.

I return to the room by the window and devour the food and gulp down the clean water. The bed looks inviting but I have work still to do and with reverence, not haste, I fill the bowl with water and using the soap, I scrub and cleanse myself of the scum of the asylum. By the time my hair, body and nails are clean the candle has burned low and like me, it has a few inches of willing left. I blow it out. The dark sits down beside me like an old friend and for the first time in an age I lie on a soft mattress and clean sheets. Sleep takes me quickly and there I dream of deliverance and a baby boy who waits for me.

There is a coach at dawn. The inn keeps its promise and wakes the yard when it must, and the horses blow steam like pipe smoke. I am dressed in the glory of clean clothes before the first tray rattles and I am at the door when the latch lifts. The innkeeper's wife gives me a parcel of bread and cheese wrapped in brown paper and tells me to keep my hands warm under the rug. "It's a long road ahead," she says, kind as a woman can be to a stranger who is not, in truth, a stranger to herself. "Branleigh Park is a piece of good fortune and it awaits you."

I thank her and lower my head so she cannot see me clear enough to describe me well. I climb into the coach and arrange my hands as I have seen ladies do, folded on the parcel as if prayer could sit still and be admired. The driver clucks to the team, the wheels take the first rut, and the road begins to do its work. Behind the hedge, a holly bough springs back into place. Far off, a rook complains and is answered by another rook with excellent manners who tells of a body waiting to be found.

The window shows me a woman in a bonnet whose ribbons sit straight and she looks out at a county she has never known and nods to it as if it had been waiting for her. I put my thumb into the palm where the little cross lies under the skin and press until the old sting wakes properly. I say, not loudly, because there is no need to wake anyone yet, "She looked like me when I was done. Or perhaps I looked like her. I could no longer tell."

The coach gains the road that will carry us south and west. The hedges thin; the sky recalls itself to duty. I tuck my chin and make myself small under the rug, and the bonnet's shadow is sufficient for now. The inn drops behind us as if it had always been a mile farther back than where I left it. "He sends me where I am meant to go," I whisper into the wool that smells of wet horse and iron and a future with a name on it: Branleigh Park. Then I sleep.

22

It was past ten when Charles Spencer found her. He had not meant to look for her. He had left his study after an hour of pacing before the hearth, the dregs of brandy untouched on his desk. The unease that gripped him felt absurd, indefinable. He told himself he merely needed air and that the strange pull between himself and the governess was nothing more than fatigue when he knew it was lust. Yet when he passed the corridor that led toward the music room and heard that fragile sob, something inside him, some old instinct to comfort, to rescue, to be needed roused like a spectre from his youth.

The door was half-open. Candlelight pooled across the parquet in a trembling sheet.

Florence sat at the pianoforte, her back to him. The single candle on the music stand burned low, its flame bowing in the draught from the open window. A draught crept through the gap, brushing her dark hair, stirring it as if with breath. Her shoulders shook, but her sobs were soundless and her hands rested in her lap, one finger tracing idle patterns against her skirt, as though she played notes no one else could hear.

Charles hesitated. He should leave. The hour was late, the

setting improper. Yet something in her fragility, the bowed head, the shimmer of tears, had snared him.

"Miss Marchwood?"

She started, turning quickly. Her eyes caught the candlelight, wide and glistening. For a moment she looked unreal, as if she had been painted there, light and shadow made flesh.

"My lord. forgive me." She rose, her voice raw. "I did not hear you."

"Why are you here alone?" he asked softly. "The fire's gone cold. You'll take a chill."

"I could not sleep," she said. "The walls of my room feel close tonight."

He glanced at the open window. Beyond it, the garden lay buried in moonlit snow. "And so you open the window to invite the winter in?" he said with a faint smile.

She gave a small, brittle laugh. "Perhaps I deserve the cold."

He frowned. "Deserve it? What nonsense is this?"

Florence sat again, clasping her hands tightly. "I am unworthy, my lord. Of this house, of its kindness. I serve, I pray, yet there are nights when the past will not loosen its grip."

Her voice trembled, and against his better judgment, he stepped nearer. "We all have troubles, Miss Marchwood. You're not alone in that."

She shook her head violently. "Not as I am. You cannot imagine it, to carry a stain so deep that even prayer turns away from it."

He moved closer, torn between pity and restraint. "You are overtired. Branleigh can feel like a prison in winter."

Her eyes lifted to his. He had never seen them like that, so bright, fevered, almost pleading. "I try to atone," she whispered. "I give every breath to the innocent. But the sin follows. It waits for me, just beyond the light."

"Miss Marchwood..."

"Florence," she said, barely audible. "Please, call me Florence."

He hesitated. "Then you must call me Charles, if it brings you comfort."

A flicker of something like joy crossed her face. "Comfort," she echoed, as if tasting the word. "I had forgotten what that is."

He could smell her now, the faintest trace of violets, the warmth of wool and woodsmoke. He had meant only to console her, but the intimacy of the moment unnerved him.

"Listen to me," he said quietly. "Whatever you've done, whatever sorrow you bear, you are not beyond forgiveness."

She gave a soft, bitter laugh. "You speak as if forgiveness were yours to give."

He tried to smile, to break the spell. "I've no such power, Miss... Florence. Only the wish to see you smile again."

And for a heartbeat, she did. The tears on her lashes caught the light like dew.

Then she reached for his hand. Her fingers were cold, startlingly so, but her touch was reverent, trembling. "You are kind," she whispered. "Too kind. I am not worthy of it."

"Please," he said, uneasy now, trying to draw back. But she held him fast.

"I would serve you always," she murmured, her voice like a vow. "You and yours. It is the only penance I know."

Before he could stop her, she bent and pressed her lips to his hand. The kiss was brief, almost chaste yet it sent a jolt through him so sharp that he felt it in his chest.

"Miss Marchwood!"

She looked up, her expression soft, untroubled. "Forgive me. I meant no offence. Only gratitude."

He stepped back, his heart hammering. The air between them vibrated with something dangerous, invisible.

"You should rest," he said, his voice unsteady. "These are

fancies brought on by the season. Tomorrow you will think differently."

She inclined her head. "Yes, my lord. Tomorrow."

But as he turned to leave, he felt her gaze follow him, silent, unwavering, until it pressed between his shoulder blades like a hand that would not let him go.

He did not sleep. The fire in his chamber had burned to a dull red glow, the coals pulsing faintly in the grate like the remnants of a young, foolish heart too stubborn to die. Charles sat at his desk, the decanter untouched, his thoughts turning in relentless circles.

It had been nothing. He told himself this again and again. A moment's lapse, merely a kindness misunderstood, a fragment of pity, no more. Such things occurred in houses like Branleigh; servants blurred into confidantes, where loneliness mistook itself for sympathy. Wiser men than he had brushed away such encounters without consequence. And yet...

The image of her refused to leave him. The candlelight on her tears, the tremor in her breath, the way her lips had grazed his hand, these details looped endlessly in his mind, too vivid to dismiss. He could still feel the faint heat of her skin, smell the faint trace of violets that clung to her.

He rose and went to the window. Outside, the gardens lay buried beneath a white stillness. The moon poured its cold light across the frozen lawns, turning every hedge and tree into sculpture. Somewhere, a branch broke under the weight of ice. He pressed his palm to the glass. The cold met him like a reprimand. He told himself it was over. That she was delicate, overwrought and that loneliness could do strange things to the mind. He would speak to Georgina in the morning, suggest a respite for the governess, perhaps a visit to family, if she had family left. The matter would resolve itself in the daylight.

But even as he thought it, he knew the truth. A line had

shifted between them. He had felt it move; felt it give way. No word of impropriety had passed even though no act had been committed. He drew his handkerchief from his pocket, similar to the one he had used to bind her finger in the garden weeks ago. He remembered how her blood had marked the cloth, a stain against the white. Had that been an omen. He stared at the pure white linen for a moment, then folded it carefully and returned it to his pocket, chaste, sinless, pious. As he crossed back to the bed, the candles flickered in his wake, their flames bowing faintly toward him and as he lay, Charles closed his eyes to the sins his eyes, his thoughts, were committing.

Far above, beneath the narrow slope of the eaves, Florence sat before the small mirror above her washstand. The candle beside her had burned to a stub, the wick trembling in its last inch of wax. In its light, her face seemed bloodless, luminous, her eyes vast and fever-bright. She touched her lips. The skin still tingled faintly where they had met his hand.

He had looked at her, truly looked for the first time. Not as a servant. Not as a governess. As a woman. The recognition had been brief but real, and such moments, she knew, were seeds. Seeds took root in darkness; they thrived on waiting.

She whispered his name once, softly, as one might whisper a prayer. Then she reached for her journal. It lay open on the table, the pages filled with her small, steady hand. She dipped the nib into the ink and began to write, her words slow and deliberate, as though taken from dictation.

This night the Lord has shown me His mercy. The walls that divide the righteous from the fallen have trembled. I am His instrument, and He directs my hand. Through me, they will learn what love demands. Through me, they will be redeemed.

She paused and held the pen poised above the page.

Somewhere below, a door creaked on its hinge, a faint sound that made her smile.

He touched me, and I am sanctified.

When the words were finished, she blotted the ink and closed the book. The covers shut with a sound like a sigh. She held it to her breast and sat, listening to the house breathe around her, the settling of beams, the quiet sigh of draughts through the chimney.

Then she rose and went to the window. Snow brushed softly against the panes, the world outside blurred and endless. The gardens below were drowned in white; the lake gleamed faintly like a sheet of glass. She placed her hand, the one that had touched him, against her cheek. Her eyes closed.

"Tomorrow," she whispered. "Tomorrow, he will remember."

The candle wavered once, twice, and went out. For a heartbeat, her reflection remained caught in the dark glass, pale, luminous, her gaze fixed on something only she could see. Then the image dissolved, and the night claimed her.

The morning crept on with a kind of brittle precision, each hour dragging behind it the weary mechanics of a household pretending stillness. Lessons were heard; the faint, dutiful rhythm of a child's recitation thudded through the ceiling like rain against a drum. A parcel came from the village bearing belated calendars from the printer, its paper freckled with melted snow. Charles shut himself in the library with the estate accounts, which he did not understand now any better than he had under his father's tutelage. Occasionally his voice could be heard summoning a footman, brisk with authority and hollow with confusion. The house went about its pantomime of order, flexed its joints, then sagged again into the heavy idleness of winter.

In her room, Georgina Spencer sat before her escritoire. The memory of the handkerchief lay spread before her like evidence awaiting judgment. She regarded the image in her mind with the same composure she had once given to scripture and to marriage, both things that had promised clarity and failed to deliver it. She chided herself not for snooping and invading the privacy of a staff member, after all the safety of her children and family was paramount. She did, however, chide the stupidity of leaving the evidence in situ rather than take it to produce as proof. Shock, that's what it had been, to find a token, her husband's monogrammed handkerchief amongst the belongings of the governess.

Instead she told herself she would retrieve it, then confront Florence within the day and Charles within the week, and herself, this she added last, knowing it to be the bravest promise and the least likely to be kept, before the season turned.

For a moment she considered marching straight to the nursery, but accusation is the theatre of the undisciplined, and she knew the governess would make the better actress. Instead, she rang for the maid.

"Clara," she said, when the girl appeared, "has Miss Marchwood asked you to tidy her room this morning?"

"Yes, my lady. But I've not been yet. Nurse sent me to the stillroom first."

"Do not go," Georgina said. "I will attend to certain matters there myself."

Clara blinked. Not impertinent, merely startled. Servants, Georgina knew, were quick to sense a shift in the air that fed them.

"Yes, my lady."

Georgina almost smiled. "And Clara, please say nothing."

The maid curtsied and withdrew, relieved to have been dismissed from mystery.

The small chamber beneath the eaves looked as it had the day before, humble, spotless, disarmingly pious. The trunk waited at the foot of the bed; its brass catch glinting. She knelt and lifted the lid with deliberate care. The evidence was gone. For an instant she thought she had misremembered, that in her confusion she had placed it elsewhere or dreamt the theft altogether. But when she straightened, she saw it peeping from the pillow, unfolded, the monogram turned upright, the faint stain of blood catching the weak daylight like a smirk.

It had been laid there purposefully, reverently like an offering at an altar.

See what we are capable of, the display said. *See what I am capable of.*

Even now, she could not deny the artistry of it. To be mocked so elegantly required genius of a kind. Her rage came clean and bright. It burned through her doubt and left only iron. Her spine remembered its design as her eyes sharpened. She folded the square roughly, thrust it into the pocket tied beneath her skirt and smoothed her gown until the fabric hid the tremor in her hands. When she turned, the doorway held a shape.

Florence Marchwood stood there, composed as ever, the soft halo of her morning cap lending her the air of an icon. She did not startle, and if she'd witnessed it, did not ask why her mistress was rifling through her belongings. She simply inclined her head and said, "My lady. You are unwell? You look pale."

The audacity of concern.

"I slept poorly," Georgina said.

"Shall I send for hartshorn? Or perhaps you would like me to sit with Lady Beatrice this afternoon. You need not exhaust yourself."

"It is no burden to attend to my husband's mother," Georgina replied evenly. "Nor is it your place to suggest otherwise."

A pause, brief, deliberate. Florence lowered her head, the

gesture smooth as a curtsy. "Forgive me. I forget myself when I am anxious for the family's welfare."

"Indeed," Georgina said. "You forget yourself frequently."

For the first time, something flickered in the governess's eyes, an infinitesimal darkening, like a shadow sliding across glass. "We all do, my lady," she said softly. "When we love."

The word settled between them like a drop of blood in clear water.

Georgina felt the collision drawing nearer, step by step, like a coach she could neither halt nor outrun. She should have spoken then. Not accusation but decree. She should have said: *You will pack. You will leave this house. You will not set eyes upon my children again.*

The sentence rose to her tongue and died there. Because she saw again the image of Theodore howling in the governess's arms, inconsolable. And she saw Charles laughing, careless, charming, unassailable, at her own outrage before or after he'd concocted a weak excuse for the handkerchief.

"Attend to your work," she said instead. "Maintain order in your own domain, that is what you are employed to do."

"Order," Florence echoed, her smile faint. "Yes. Order."

As Georgina moved past her, the governess shifted just enough to permit passage and their sleeves brushed. The touch sent a jolt through Georgina, sharp and intimate as a whispered blasphemy. She did not look back.

The rest of the morning unspooled with a dreadful exactness. Hattie recited the Kings of Israel in a voice so small it might have been prayer. Florence prompted gently, each mild correction wrapped in silk. Theodore slept, milk damp on his lips. Downstairs, Beatrice dozed over her Bible, her finger marking a verse she would never finish. Charles sent word that he meant to ride when the weather cleared and would Georgina kindly review the stable accounts before luncheon. She took the note, folded it, and dropped it into the fire.

Through it all, the handkerchief dragged at her consciousness like a secret stitched into her hem. She could feel it pressing through the pocket cloth, branding her thigh with its hidden monogram and stain. The thought of Florence discovering its absence, of that quiet, knowing smile, of the handkerchief laid out like a relic made her stomach twist with something perilously close to awe.

The house held its quiet too tightly, like a mouth suppressing words. Servants moved with unnatural precision, sensing weather that had not yet broken. The cook snapped at the scullery maid; the scullery maid slammed pans as if to remind the kitchen that metal, at least, was honest. In the laundry, the steam rose and hung in the air like a congregation of unshriven souls. From the nursery came a faint hum. No words just the tune. The same tune that had drifted through the house for weeks, patient as a curse that no prayer could banish.

Georgina stood at her window and looked out upon the garden. The snow lay clean, deceptive, its purity the cruellest of disguises. Across the white stretch of lawn, a single trail of footprints marked the rose walk – dark, distinct, deliberate. She knew whose they were. And she knew where those feet meant to lead the house if no hand stopped them.

What remained, then, was choice. A woman's choices are always the same: to speak and be dismissed as hysteric, to keep silent and be pitied as fool. But there was a third path, one she had long ignored, one unbecoming of the well-bred. To act.

She turned from the window. The light was thinning now, the kind that bleaches colour from everything it touches. On her escritoire, beneath a neat stack of correspondence, sat the small drawer that held her private instruments of authority: keys, docket, sealing wax, and a single roll of good London paper, unadorned, unanswerable. She drew it open.

She would write. Not to the agency who had failed to reply to Beatrice, but to her cousin Margaret in town, whose husband's position on half a dozen charitable boards gave him a reach far greater than his intellect. Margaret's parlour was a thoroughfare of discreet information, where scandal could be sifted from mere rumour. Facts, if handled properly, could be coaxed into daylight.

Yes. She would write today. She would send the note by one of the boys from the Home Farm, a quiet, trustworthy creature who owed her a favour and could be persuaded by a coin. She would... A knock interrupted her. Not timid, not intrusive; precise, deliberate. The kind of knock that announces ownership, not request.

"Enter," she said, and schooled her face into composure before the latch turned.

Florence Marchwood stood in the doorway, a ledger clasped to her breast. It might have been a book or a weapon; in her hands, it was both.

"The nursery tallies for your review, my lady," she said, her tone perfectly modulated. "Mrs. Dobbs asked that I deliver them."

Georgina extended her hand. Florence did not move closer. The two women regarded one another across the measured space of the room. To an unknowing eye, it might have looked like ordinary civility, a mistress and her servant, dividing the day's business. But beneath the harmless words and inaction, something else passed between them, a claim, a challenge, a subtle transfer of dominion. Florence reached out and passed the ledger.

Georgina didn't quite snatch the book as take it forcefully. "Thank you."

Florence's gaze dipped briefly to the pocket of Georgina's gown where, if one were reckless enough to guess, the outline of a folded handkerchief might be imagined. When she looked up again, her expression was mild. "Is there anything further you require, my lady?"

"Yes," Georgina said. The word surprised her. "I require that you remember your place."

Florence inclined her head, her smile small and immaculate. "Always."

Georgina's voice sharpened. "Do not mistake my silence for consent or weakness, I am merely biding my time."

A pause, thin as a blade.

"I would never mistake it so," Florence said softly. Then, after a heartbeat: "Nor expect anything more."

The air between them tightened. The collision had not yet occurred, but the imaginary carriages were already visible upon the road, the drivers fixed in their course, the horses beginning to quicken their stride. The taste of iron lay on the back of Georgina's tongue. Florence turned and left. The door closed without sound, but the quiet that followed was worse than noise,not relief, not reprieve, but the poised stillness of a theatre moments before the curtain rises.

Georgina sank into her chair. The handkerchief pressed its small, accusing weight against her hip. She opened the ledger to a page of orderly figures and fixed her eyes upon them until the rhythm of the numbers calmed her pulse. But she did not deceive herself. Numbers were obedient because they could afford to be. People were not.

The inevitable would not come with thunder, thunder announces itself via streaks of white in the sky. It would come like the tide, soft at first, an innocent cooling about the ankles. Then the drag. Then, before one could cry out, the ground gone beneath the feet.

23

The snow had fallen without pause through the night, until Branleigh Park lay drowned beneath it in a white silence so complete it seemed less weather than shroud. The house crouched under its weight, windows glazed opaque, chimneys breathing faintly against the pale sky. Inside, the air hung thick with coal dust and restraint. The servants moved like echoes, their voices subdued, their steps deliberate, as though the house itself had forbidden any sound that might wake whatever malice slept within its walls.

Lady Beatrice Spencer sat in her usual chair by the window of her chamber, wrapped in shawls that did little to warm her failing body. The garden beyond was a blur of frost and memory. Once she had walked there, hand in hand with her son, a toddler then a child, quick and laughing. Now only the crows kept vigil. Her hands, folded in her lap, looked more bone than flesh. Yet there was purpose in her stillness. She was not resting. She was waiting.

For weeks she had tried to dismiss her unease as age, as nerves, as the ordinary fears of a woman too long confined to her own company. But small dissonances had begun to gather like dust: the drowned doll, the letter ignored, the governess's soft voice humming after dark, the baby's unnatural quiet, Hattie's dark looks. Each detail alone was nothing. Together, they formed the shape of dread. And dread, once given form, demands action.

That morning she had summoned Mrs. Dobbs. "Fetch more linen from the upper corridor, my bed need attending to," she said, her tone mild to hide her shame.

The housekeeper nodded and made to leave then Beatrice asked. "Where is the governess and the children?"

"I believe they are taking some air while the snow has stopped. A turn around the rose garden. They have just left."

Beatrice persisted, the time for subtlety gone. "Do you have a key for the governess's room?"

Mrs. Dobbs hesitated. "Miss Marchwood keeps that room locked now, my lady. She is particular about her things."

"Indeed," Beatrice replied, her voice sharpening. "Then I must be particular too. Bring me the key. I trust you have a spare."

Mrs. Dobbs had assured Beatrice that she did and then obeyed, trembling, lantern in hand. The climb to the eaves had left Beatrice breathless, her heart stuttering like a faulty clock. But she pressed on, unwilling to appear frail before the woman who had managed her household since her youth and was fit as a fiddle. At the top, Beatrice took the key and asked Mrs. Dobbs to remain outside.

When the key turned and the door yielded, the light revealed nothing that should have unsettled her, and yet everything did. The room was spotless, monastic, too precise in its order. The narrow bed was made with military care. The small desk gleamed but it was the trunk at the foot of the bed that drew her. The latch lifted easily and inside lay a few folded garments, a ribboned bundle of letters, and beneath them, a neat sheaf of newspaper clippings.

The first was from *The Buckingham Advertiser*, dated two years prior. The paper was soft with handling; the edges browned like old parchment.

TRAGEDY AT RAVENBROOKE ASYLUM

Fire in Female Ward.

Several Dead, Four Patients Missing

Beneath the headline was a crude engraving of a long building engulfed in smoke. Beatrice's breath caught. She remembered that spring and the talk at parish teas, the speculation whispered in pews. The women who escaped into the woods. Some found, raving. Others simply gone.

Her eyes fell upon a name buried in the small print: *Among the unaccounted-for are three attendants and four patients, described as unstable and dangerous.* Four. She turned to the next clipping.

Search Abandoned for Missing Inmate, Emily Leonard

Formerly daughter of a clergyman, committed after the death of her infant.

Considered melancholic and violent. Believed deceased after the unidentifiable body of a woman was found.

The letters seemed to dance before her eyes. *Emily Leonard.* The name stirred a faint, dreadful echo of a sermon heard long ago, a vicar's lament for a fallen parishioner. Beatrice lowered the paper to her lap. The room tilted slightly around her. Florence

Marchwood. Emily Leonard. The governess's pale hands. Her measured voice. The way she spoke of sin as though she'd shaken hands with it. Her devotion to Theodore.

It could not be, and yet the possibility lodged in her like a splinter beneath skin. She returned the clippings to the trunk, closing the lid with care. Her fingers trembled against the brass. By the time she reached her room again, the resolve had settled in her like a stone.

That night the house lay still as burial. The fire in her grate spat weakly, casting red veins across the walls. Beatrice sat upright among her pillows, her breath shallow but steady. She could summon Charles or she could confide in Georgina. But she would not. Her son's blindness to danger and a pretty face had always been his vice, and Georgina's sense of propriety would only dull the blade. No this confrontation belonged to her.

"Clara," she said when the maid entered. "Send for Miss Marchwood. Tell her I wish to speak before she retires."

The girl hesitated. "At this hour, my lady?"

"At this hour."

Florence came quickly. Always prompt, always composed. She entered with a candle in hand and closed the door softly behind her. Her cheeks were touched by the glow of the nursery fire, her eyes calm, unreadable.

"You sent for me, my lady?"

"Sit," Beatrice said, pointing to the chair.

Florence obeyed, folding her hands like a penitent.

"I have lived long enough," Beatrice began, her voice thin but steady, "to know when shadows lie upon a house. You brought yours here with you."

A flicker crossed Florence's face, not fear, but recognition. "I don't understand."

Beatrice's hand tightened on the coverlet. "Do not lie. I have seen what you keep in your trunk. The clippings. *Ravenbrooke.*"

The name hung in the air. The candle kept it's nerve.

Florence drew a breath, slow, deliberate. "You went into my room."

"I did," Beatrice said. "And I found what you meant me not to see."

The governess's expression softened. She looked at Beatrice with something close to pity. "You should not have done that," she said quietly.

"Tell me the truth," Beatrice whispered. "Who are you?"

Florence rose and crossed to the window. Snow glowed pale against the glass, washing her features in spectral light. "I was wronged," she said softly. "You think me wicked, but I am not. They punished me for grieving. They called me mad because I prayed to my dead child. My father..." Her voice caught. "He was a man of God. He beat me for my prayers and my sin and caused the death of my baby."

Beatrice felt the tremor of pity return, unwelcome but irrepressible.

Florence turned, her face wet with tears. "The Lord saw me," she said. "He knew my suffering. The fire was His mercy. His cleansing. He set me free. And He sent me here, to love, to serve, to begin again."

Beatrice's heart faltered. "You poor, broken creature," she murmured, extending a trembling hand. "No one should suffer such cruelty."

Florence knelt beside the bed, taking the old woman's hand and pressing it to her lips. "You are kind," she whispered. "Kind as a mother."

For a moment, Beatrice's fear ebbed. But then Florence lifted her head, and the change came, subtle, then seismic. The tears were gone. The softness vanished. What looked back at her was calm, certain, invincible.

"I'm not broken, my lady," she said, her voice smooth as polished stone. "I'm healed."

The words were a benediction and a threat both.

Beatrice recoiled. "Healed?"

"By His fire," Florence said simply. "I am His servant now. And I keep His house."

The silence between them swelled until it felt alive.

Beatrice found her voice at last. "Safe," she whispered. "Is that what you call this?"

Florence smiled with that same small, tranquil smile that had deceived them all. "Especially with me here."

She rose, curtsied, and left, her candle trailing a small golden wake through the dark.

Beatrice sat rigid, her heart hammering against her ribs. The scent of lavender and ash clung to the air as did the words in the clipping. *Patients still missing.* Beatrice's lungs constricted as pain seared across her chest and her pulse raced beyond control, sending her into a panic that had her reaching for the pull cord which summoned Clara. Afraid to be alone and knowing she could not disturb her son and Georgina at this ungodly hour, when the maid arrived she asked her to sit a while, until sleep granted her peace from her woes. Then, in the morning she would tell all, and have that wolf in sheep's clothing banished by midday. She would never forget the look in the eye of the beast, yet the memory of it had served a purpose, brought resolve and strength. It would live a few hours more, until the morning.

Snow thickened, closing the world with the quiet of a hand over a child's eyes. It settled on sills and roofs until the terraces looked like pale causeways and the urns on the balustrade brimmed. Chapel, stables, glasshouse, and the long south front with its watchful panes slept beneath the same immaculate pall. The house breathed slowly, as if the drifts had laid a cool cloth to its brow and soothed it into forgetting.

Within, the last scuttle of coal had been tipped upon the last grate; servants' talk dwindled to yawns, then to the soft collapse of straw mattresses. Even the clocks kept time more discreetly, unwilling to wake the sleeping. A loosened shutter clicked once, found no answer, and was still.

In Lady Beatrice Spencer's chamber, a candle made a small church of light. Its circle laid patient arches upon the ceiling and set the bedposts to keeping vigil. A Bible lay open where an old hand had held its place and withdrawn, the thin paper shining with a faint rim of gilt like frost on hedge. Beside it, spectacles waited, folded as if their owner had gone into the next room to fetch a word and would presently return to read it.

Clara had been kindly dismissed after falling asleep sitting upright. Beatrice dozed rather than slept, the art age bestows when true sleep grows rare. Memories walked the corridors of her mind and moved a chair here, opened a cupboard there, yet her doze had gentleness. Pillows had learned the stoop of her spine and a shawl lay over her shoulders with the exactness of a well-trained maid. Now and then her breath rattled like a moth against a shade, then quieted. When the candle leaned, she leaned; when it steadied, she steadied too.

The latch lifted without the sound a latch should make. Such things can be taught discretion. The door opened by inches. The draught entered first and made its curtsey to the flame then a slender figure followed, moving with the same unswerving quiet and right to belong. Bare feet kissed the rug and left no print. The hair was braided and bound, the braid lying like a dark stole. No candle. None was needed. The room offered its geometry as if it had been sketched in a private notebook.

Florence Marchwood paused on the threshold and listened. Not the listening of guilt; she had drilled that out of herself. The listening of someone who treats a house as an instrument with strings. A distant pipe sighed, an oak beam settled at the change in air, otherwise nothing. She closed the door. The latch consented and kept her secret.

The light arranged her face for the room to see it composed, almost serene, no admission of drama. She might have been a nurse to test a poultice, a dutiful daughter come to kiss a mother who had waited up too long. Colour in the cheeks was winter's doing. The eyes were clear. She did not look at the Bible. She did not look at Beatrice at once. She looked at the pillow where a head should rest, then away, as if to prove haste was not a god she served.

She drew the curtain an inch. Outside, snow went about its work with monastic patience. Florence watched for two slow breaths, let the curtain fall, and turned. She came to the bed and stood until the old woman's breathing entered her own. Beatrice's face had been made finer by sleep, the mouth unarmed, the old valour folded like a uniform on a chair. Florence smiled then, small and private, the smile one gives a task long prepared and now to be done without fuss.

She folded her hands and sang softly, so quietly the words were barely audible. It was little more than breath shaped into a tune. No words at first, only their contour, so familiar the air seemed to lean toward what would be asked. The melody had drifted through this house for months, laid itself beneath doors and upon pillows, become a property of brass bells and iron latches, until objects knew it as well as people. The sound found the candle and made it bow to words altered slightly.

"Sleep beneath the roses, now," she sang, each word set

down like a petal rather than dropped. "Sleep, for your time has come."

Beatrice stirred. Lids fluttered; the mouth worked at a name not safe for dark rooms. Her eyes opened and took in the coarse facts of ceiling and carving before they caught the figure at the bedside and held fast, as if the iris were a net and had trapped a fish.

"Miss..." The voice was a draught at first. She cleared her throat. "Miss Marchwood?"

"Hush," Florence said, and the hush was prescription rather than rule as her hands moved in the dark. "It is late, my lady. You must rest."

Beatrice's hand moved on the coverlet, searching but not finding the bell-rope that had been moved out of reach. "Why are you here?" She meant sternness. Only humanity came.

"To pray for you," Florence answered. She smiled again, a fixed, cool brightness. "To sing you safe to the next life."

Beatrice's breath shortened and made the moth-sound once more. "I have prayed enough. If you have any mercy, go."

"I do," Florence said softly. "I have mercy. And duty."

Her fingers touched the pillow's edge, not snatching, simply taking hold as a seamstress grips cloth she means to cut true. She lifted it with both hands. Feathers sighed like a remembered field. She leaned forward, tidy and unhurried.

The first touch was a benediction. The old eyes widened, not with theatre but with the injured surprise of a body confronted by an absurdity: the instrument of rest turned to an instrument of ending. Hands came up, slow hands, robbed for years of seconds they now sorely needed. They slid along ticking, found the firmness beneath and pushed. Florence's hands replied, steady, containing, the way one steadies a frightened child who might fall.

"Sleep," she whispered into the lullaby's current. "Sleep, Mother. You will wake to better light."

The struggle was soft. Bodies nearly finished with their business do not fling themselves about. Beatrice turned her head a fraction and the pillow followed. She tried to speak and made the sound of an small animal. The candle stretched thin, drew itself together, stretched again. Gilt on the Bible caught and gave back a prickle of light, like frost under an early foot.

It did not take long. That is a mercy and should be recognised when it comes. Breath that had been a moth became a thread, then a thread cut on a dull edge, then silence. The hands forgot their purpose. The eyes forgot their task. A heart that had outlasted infants and fashions and a husband's smiles found an hour that required nothing more. Outside, the snow deepened. This too was fact.

Florence held the pillow a while longer, listening for an answer to a foreign prayer. When she lifted it, she smoothed the crease with a mother's palm and set it straight. The face below had altered, its vigilant sorrow eased, the features pared back to their idea. Death is an honest editor. She replaced the pillow then arranged the hands upon the chest, thumb to thumb, careful as if balancing a cross. The wedding ring gave a brief gold wink like a fish turning under ice and went dull. She kissed the brow. Not a lover's kiss. A rite.

"You were the only one who saw me," she said.

The room received this without commentary. Things learn quickly when to be silent. The candle applied itself to the work of continuing. Florence drew the coverlet to the shoulders with an attentiveness that would have pleased a stern physician. She straightened the Bible and laid the spectacles upon it, arm aligned to arm, so that the dead, glancing back, might know order had not been driven out. She turned to go.

At the door she looked back once, the only indulgence she

allowed within the ceremony. Beatrice lay as a good grandmother should in her last hour: composed, folded, honoured. The candle kept its office. She opened the door and let the trapped draught escape. The corridor accepted her without surprise. She passed beneath the family portraits, and each painted face regarded her, tried and failed to place her in its ledger of guilt, then looked away.

Near the nursery landing she stopped. The stillness there was different, not silence, but a pulse muffled beneath the skin of the house. She listened. Through the crack in the door came a faint exhalation of warmth, the breath of the living rooms she had tended so faithfully. Theodore slept inside; she could hear it, the soft, mechanical rhythm of a child's lungs learning the world by repetition. Each breath was a defiance of the one that had just ceased upstairs.

Hattie turned in her bed and sighed, that small, unconscious sound children make to prove to the dark that in sleep it holds no fear. Florence placed her palm flat upon the panel. The wood was warm, the warmth of ordinary life and folk, the earth, breathing. It confirmed her purpose.

"Sleep beneath the roses, child," she whispered, not singing now. Music is sometimes a kindness, sometimes a lie, and tonight she needed neither. "Sleep and fear no more."

She moved on. Her shadow drifted beside her, unhurried. She never hurried. She had not hurried at the inn, nor at the lake. Haste betrays the heart; haste confesses. Her room beneath the eaves received her as it always did, with its narrow bed and small, watchful mirror. She shut the door and turned the key, an act of habit, not caution. The floor beneath her was cold. In one of her lives she had been taught that purity follows performance, that the priest must cleanse his hands before he leaves the altar. At the washstand she performed that rite then returned to her desk and opened her journal. The page waited, blank and welcoming. She dipped the nib, and the ink answered her with its small, obedient scratch.

Mercy has visited the house. The old pain is quieted. A watchful eye has been asked to rest. She blotted the words. The paper drank them greedily, as snow drinks sound. Downstairs, the clocks resumed their patient arithmetic, counting time as though nothing in the world had changed. Morning would find the snow higher on the garden urns, the chapel bell ringing once by human hand rather than accident, the kitchen maid coaxing the frozen pump with a pail of boiling water. Life, indifferent, tireless, would resume its domestic routine.

Behind her, the room she had left downstairs cooled into stillness. A life had ended without struggle, as if the world, often graceless, had remembered civility at last. Florence set down her pen and placed her palms flat on the desk. The bones beneath the skin protested faintly, small reminders that she, too, was still among the living. She blew out the candle. The dark settled with the intimacy of breath. Her eyes remained open, her lips parted in the shape of no word at all. When she prayed, it was in the private dialect she had made for herself, one that Heaven no longer recognised and Hell had grown too weary to translate.

24

Dawn entered Branleigh Park like a penitent, slow, colourless, and bowed beneath the burden of snow. The light had thinned to transparency, confessing rather than illuminating. Overnight, the drifts had climbed the terraces, hemming the lawns in white lace. The house itself seemed to breathe beneath its burial cloth, half-asleep, half-listening.

The first sounds were hesitant: the cough of a kitchen fire coaxed from embers, the shy clink of a coal scuttle, the cautious shuffle of boots unwilling to disturb the hush. Before the clocks had struck their first note, sorrow had already taken its place in the corridors, patient as an undertaker waiting for the family to understand.

It was Clara who found her. She came with the morning draught and a small posset scented faintly with nutmeg, the ritual offering of a day that expected to be ordinary. She murmured her customary brightness, "Good morning, my lady," and laid the tray upon the table. When no reply came, she turned, saw the hands folded just so, and froze. The skin had already begun to cool and the peace upon the face was too complete to be mistaken. Clara fled, her apron clutched to her mouth, a sound escaping that woke the corridor more cleanly than any bell.

The fragile machinery of morning collapsed. The butler ran, coat half-buttoned as Mrs. Dobbs, the housekeeper, crossed herself once before issuing orders like commands in battle.

"Fetch the doctor, the vicar, and Mr. Yates from the village, he's the one for the laying-out. And mind the road, mind it." She turned to the maids. "Coffee, strong. Broth to hand. Not a tear where the family may see you."

Then, to the one who broke at once, she gave a quick hug that smelled of soap and starch. The household, trained for duty, startled by its usefulness moved as one body newly awake to grief.

Georgina heard the stir from her dressing room and knew before the words reached her. Grief has its own grammar that the body reads without translation. She went bareheaded down the corridor, her hair unpinned, pins biting at her nape. For once, she did not compose herself. When she entered and saw the truth, the shawl folded neatly, the Bible, the spectacles waiting as if their owner had stepped out for a moment her composure failed as gracefully as glass shatters.

"Oh, Mama," she said, and the title slid into tenderness. She knelt, kissed the still hand, and felt the ancient wish rise: *take mine instead*. But the dead do not bargain only keep what they have purchased.

Charles came quickly when called. Grief stripped him of his easy varnish, leaving the boy beneath. He stood at the foot of the bed, as he had done long ago when Beatrice had scolded and forgiven him for trampling her flower beds. He touched her cheek with a tenderness that seemed borrowed from another man. His eyes, which had rarely known purpose, found it now too late. When he turned, Florence was already there.

She had entered without sound, as angels in sentimental

paintings are imagined to do, arriving by inevitability rather than by door. Her dark gown, plain but immaculate, caught what little light remained. Her face was tranquil, her hands bare.

"I came to offer help," she said softly.

To Georgina, the words struck like a bruise but to Charles, they were mercy itself. He let her move. Florence fed the fire, straightened the coverlet, and at Mrs. Dobbs nod, slipped away. She returned with tea, sweetened more than necessary, because grief asks for sugar and offered the cups with calm precision.

"Weeping may endure for a night," she murmured, "but joy cometh in the morning." Not sermon, not comfort simply the sound of scripture arranged to fill the air until thought could return.

The doctor arrived, detained by snow. He confirmed what everyone knew with the ritual watch held to the wrist. "Peaceful," he said, a word that costs nothing and is seldom contradicted. The vicar followed, bringing with him a wisp of cold that made the candles tremble. He read the prayers, commended the soul, and asked the living to be good because the dead could no longer manage it.

By noon, mourning had been achieved. Black crepe flowered through the house. The mirrors were veiled, the pianoforte closed. The children were dressed for the occasion, Hattie restless beneath her ribbon, Theodore pouting at the feel of new fabric. And Florence, tireless, moved among them. She wept where weeping was expected, but never to disfigure. She guided Hattie's small hand to place a sprig of rosemary on the sheet. She carried Theodore with a serene possessiveness, his head beneath her chin, his breath warming her throat. She brewed tea, poured cups, divided grief into practical errands.

Charles noticed and his notice became gratitude. To be spared the mechanics of mourning was its own benediction. "You are an angel among us," he told her, and believed it.

Georgina saw the same gesture and instead saw performance. The still hands, the perfect pitch of verse, the careful modesty, it was a role, and Florence had rehearsed it well. Beatrice had spoken her fear and concerns and now Georgina beheld its consequence dressed as virtue pouring tea. She looked at her husband and knew that truth, once again, would make her monstrous.

When the undertaker came, necessity resumed command. The dead were clothed for their second debut. Beatrice, composed beneath white linen, seemed to have selected the expression herself, serene, dignified, certain. Candles turned the chamber into a chapel. Visitors came in a slow procession through the park: villagers, tenants, the rector's wife. They spoke of her patience, her generosity, her faith, each quality measured by how deeply they wished it to reflect upon their own souls.

The funeral came swiftly and within days. The chapel filled with cold breath and hesitant steps. A spray of lilies, forced into bloom by hothouse cruelty, perfumed the air to the edge of nausea. The rector spoke well, steadfast, charitable, long-suffering. The words clinked like coins in an old collection plate.

Florence wept then, beautifully. She stood at the aisle's end, one child in each arm, black against white stone, the image of perfect maternity. When the coffin passed, she bent her head, her cheek against Hattie's hair. The sight struck through the congregation like a light through glass. Men blinked; women adjusted their gloves. Even Mrs. Dobbs dabbed her eyes with the same kerchief she kept for onions and funerals.

Charles saw salvation in that tableau. His household whole, preserved, the living soothed. He pressed Georgina's hand, seeking agreement. Her fingers lay cold and still in his.

To Georgina, the picture was accusation. The congregation's gaze slid to Florence as if she were the widow instead of the servant. The world forgives deceit when it is wept with grace and it punishes suspicion in a woman who does not. She bit down on silence, feeling it draw blood. There would be an hour for truth but not yet.

The cortege wound back through the park, black upon white, a signature against snow. The drifts filled behind them, erasing the record as fast as it was written.

In the nursery windows, a faint glow burned, a story already forming for the children that that grandmothers go to heaven, that heaven is kind, that lullabies mean safety. Florence returned and restored the house to motion. She directed the servants with quiet authority, supervised the tea, murmured psalms in the correct key. To the villagers she was sanctity itself; to the household, law incarnate; to Charles, solace; to Georgina, a mask she longed to tear from the face that wore it so well.

By evening, the house had subsided into the weary stillness that follows ritual. Candles dwindled, corridors cooled, and the snow leaned heavier against the doors. In the Dowager's room, the bed was stripped bare. In the nursery, a woman in faux mourning rocked a sleeping child, humming without words. At her window, Georgina watched the blank garden. Somewhere beneath the white, a fox or something of the woods moved lightly on invisible paws. The print it left was too delicate to frighten anyone who did not know how to appreciate the wild.

She did not speak the word that rose in her throat. She let it rest there instead, bitter as medicine. Then she closed the curtain and turned back to the room where grief had dressed her, and the long war, already begun, waited for its first sound.

The house had woken to tragedy. By evening, it had remembered its training. Grief was folded into linen, pressed flat beneath duty. Fires were tended, doors latched, trays carried with a reverence that was half exhaustion. The corridors, which had trembled with voices that morning, grew calm again, their hush restored like order after a riot.

And yet beneath every murmured prayer, beneath every cup of sweetened tea that passed from hand to trembling hand, something lingered. It moved beneath the skin of the house, too patient to be called hunger, too knowing to be called peace. It watched as curtains were drawn and candles pinched, as the living rehearsed their civility around the newly dead.

It waited, as certain of its hour as the tide is certain of the moon.

25

The house had entered mourning, and yet something deeper than grief had taken root.

In the days following the funeral, *Branleigh Park* grew quieter than death alone could account for. It was not the hush of sorrow but of listening, walls attuned to whispers, carpets holding the memory of each step. The curtains hung half-drawn, the air heavy with beeswax and camphor, the scent of preservation rather than life. The Dowager's rooms were locked, the key hidden in Mrs. Dobbs's desk, but still her presence drifted through the house like a perfume that refused to fade. The faint tick of her clock persisted on the landing; a trace of lavender trembled in doorways; a chill stirred nightly at the stair's base, as though her skirts brushed past.

Yet grief, like snow, does not last. It settles, it conceals, and beneath its weight something new begins to grow. Into that space, silent, sanctified, expectant, *Florence Marchwood* began to bloom. Her ascendancy was quiet. It came dressed in usefulness. She oversaw the children's mealtimes when Georgina seemed locked in grief. She reminded the cook of broth for the master's cough, suggested extra blankets for the grooms, drafted

Charles's correspondence in her elegant, God-fearing hand. Small acts, every one of them, and all applauded.

"She keeps us from falling to pieces," Charles said one evening before the fire, his tone softened by gratitude that felt perilously close to need.

Across from him, Georgina's needle paused above her embroidery frame. "You speak as though the household were an orphan," she said lightly. "Mrs. Dobbs is hardly incompetent."

"She's capable enough," he replied, "but she's not Miss Marchwood. There's a steadiness in her, a grace under trial. We're fortunate to have her."

Georgina pricked her finger, watched the bead of blood rise and glisten like a small, accusing eye. "Fortunate," she repeated.

Florence's steadiness soon became the rhythm by which the house breathed. Servants deferred to her without realising it. The nursemaid sought her approval before dressing the children. The gardener waited for her nod before cutting winter roses. Even Mrs. Dobbs lowered her tone in the governess's presence, as though addressing visiting nobility.

No one could say precisely when Florence ceased to defer and began to reign. It was not in words, it was in the easy confidence of gestures, in silences so full they erased others. Georgina would enter a room to find Florence already there: Hattie upon her knee, the child's pale hair lit by firelight, the governess's voice wrapping scripture around them like silk. Or Florence rocking Theodore with that slow, private rhythm that turned a duty into devotion.

Charles would pause at the threshold, drawn as if to prayer. He watched the pair, the mother displaced, the interloper enthroned, and his face softened in a way Georgina had not seen for years. And yet she still didn't act, be it from uncertainty, the debilitating grief that had consumed her, or the lack of love for her husband that evaporated daily, like steam from a kettle. The melancholy that wrapped itself around her was an enemy impossible to shrug off and in the same moment, it was a companion she could rely on not to leave her side. Georgina often felt quite mad and often gloriously calm as though nothing could penetrate the barrier she was building around her heart. Even when she witnessed things a wife should not, hurt barely registered.

"Forgive me, my lord," Florence would murmur, modestly rising. "The little ones were restless."

"You needn't apologise," he would say, lingering still. "It does me good to hear peace in this house again."

From the shadows of the doorway, Georgina would watch herself vanish by degrees. Wife into bystander. Lover, companion, bearer of heirs, becoming a fine mist. She signed accounts in her careful hand, dined when summoned, smiled when expected but the pulse of Branleigh no longer answered to her. The house had found a new heart, and it beat quietly beneath the governess's calm.

The evenings altered first. Charles took his meals in his study more often where Florence attended him with tea and books. Once, passing by the half-closed door, Georgina heard laughter, the harmony of two voices, mingled.

Florence's was soft, low, and tuned to the key of temptation.

"You have an old soul, Miss Marchwood," Charles said. "A rare woman who can quote Milton and mend stockings in the same breath."

Florence's reply floated out, gentle and sure. "The scriptures tell us there is a time to speak and a time to sew, my lord. I try to honour both."

"And the Lord," he said, amused, "must be very pleased with you."

Georgina turned away, trembling. Later she would tell herself she had misheard the tenderness in his tone, that gratitude could sound like longing if one listened from the wrong doorway. But the sound stayed with her, an echo that soured everything it touched.

The servants whispered too, though softly and without malice. "There's something holy about her," the cook said. "The master looks ten years younger when she enters."

Mrs. Dobbs pursed her lips. "Holy or something passing for it," she said, and replaced the teapot lid too hard.

Even the vicar spoke of her after calling to offer condolences. "A woman of uncommon grace," he told the butler on his departure, "chastened by sorrow but untouched by it."

And so it spread, the legend of *Miss Marchwood of Branleigh Park*, the saintly governess, the comforter of children, the keeper of the bereaved. Only Georgina knew the truth, or the truth as her nerves spelled it. She saw beneath the calm a hunger polished to respectability, a fervour too exact to be harmless. She saw how Florence's eyes lingered on Charles, not boldly, but with the composure of one already certain of her place or where her place may one day be. She saw how her daughter's fingers clung to the governess's skirt, how Theodore's cries ceased at her touch, how even the dogs wagged when she passed.

And she saw, most cruelly, how her husband's indifference began to resemble displeasure.

When she dared to speak, to ask whether Florence's sermons were now to replace conversation, Charles sighed as though wounded. "Must everything be accusation? Miss Marchwood has been a blessing. You might learn from her patience."

"Her patience," Georgina repeated, tasting the word. "Or her piety?"

He looked up from his papers, frowning. "Perhaps both."

It was the first time in years she wished to strike him and it was only the knowledge of gentlewomen being spirited away to institutions that counselled her. She would not be one of those women who played into the hands of a husband who was waiting for the right time and a good excuse to unburden himself. That night she sat in the dark long after the candles had burned down, listening. Above her head came the faint creak of boards, the soft, measured pacing of a woman who held the night as her dominion. Florence's footsteps, steady as prayer. Even sleep, it seemed, now answered to her.

That night, *Florence dreamed.* The room was Beatrice's or seemed so at first. The scent of lavender hung faint and stale beneath the darker trace of ash. The candle on the table stuttered, the flame bent double as though listening. Outside, the snow pressed at the windowpanes, patient as breath upon glass.

She stood at the bedside, the pillow in her hands, its weight both slight and sacred. Her own breathing filled the room, measured, deliberate, the rhythm of someone performing a rite already learned by heart. But when she looked down, it was not the Dowager's face that met her. It was Georgina's. The younger woman's eyes stared up, clear, glistening, startled not by pain but by knowledge. Her mouth moved beneath the feathers, shaping a word that could not escape. Recognition passed between them like spirit to medium.

Florence pressed harder. "*Sleep, my lady,*" she whispered, her voice all balm and benediction. "*You'll wake in a better world.*"

The body struggled once, twice, then yielded. And into that stillness flowed something vast and unspeakably sweet, *relief*, yes, but also release, like the final resolving of discord into perfect, devout harmony. When she woke, her pulse was steady. Her skin cool. The dream lay behind her not as memory but as promise kept in miniature. She turned her head. Dawn had begun its pale confession at the edge of the sky, the faint grey pressing at the window like a timid visitor. She watched it gather itself, this weak light, and felt within her a peace so pure it might have been joy.

Florence smiled. The house would wake soon, almost her house now, though the world had yet to call it so. Each room would open its eyes to her governance. Each voice would soften in her presence. The children would rise, obedient as prayers. Charles would descend the stairs with that new, unguarded gratitude she had taught him to feel. All would be well. *All was already well.*

She rose, tied her robe, and crossed to the washstand. The freezing water bit her fingers, a small, exquisite mortification. She welcomed it. Purity was pain rightly placed.

Kneeling, she began the day's prayers, her voice low and even, the syllables moving across her tongue like beads through fingers. "*Create in me a clean heart, O Lord,*" she murmured, eyes half-closed. "*And renew a right spirit within me.*"

Below, the first bell rang, the soft toll that marked the servants' waking. Branleigh Park stirred. And Florence Marchwood, governess, redeemer, saint, lifted her face to the ashen light and smiled into the dawn.

26

By early spring, *Branleigh Park* had found its rhythm again or at least the convincing imitation of one. The shutters were raised, the fires coaxed into cheer, and even the servants' laughter, uncertain, like a child reciting lessons, returned to the kitchen. The world beyond the iron gates, seeing smoke rise neatly from every chimney, would have said that mourning had passed. But beneath that fragile choreography, the house had altered its orbit. Its gravity had shifted. And all things, voices, glances, hearts, now turned toward a single, quiet sun. *Florence Marchwood.*

The mourning silks were folded away. Georgina had insisted on it, though the insistence sounded more like surrender. "My mother would not have wished us to wear sorrow forever," she said.

Charles, distracted by papers he did not read, murmured agreement. Florence, standing nearby, lowered her lashes. The black gown of servitude had been replaced by one of dove-grey wool, soft as smoke, modest as virtue. Her dominion began with kindness, *as all lasting dominions do.*

She anticipated before she asked. She reminded, soothed,

arranged. She sent blankets to the stables before frost could threaten, placed broth upon the master's tray before the cough could deepen. She wrote to the vicar, to the steward, to the upholsterer, always in the same gentle hand with each word an act of service, each act a quiet stone in the foundation of her reign.

At first, the household obeyed from habit. It was natural, after all, to defer to one who seemed to remember the Dowager's will more precisely than the Dowager herself ever had. More precisely than Georgina, even. Then habit ripened into reverence. Florence no longer waited upon instruction. She simply did and her doing remade the house.

It was Florence who supervised the polishing of silver. Florence who approved the nursery's fire. Florence who inspected the linen with eyes that found fault without ever raising their voice. Each gesture was couched in humility. Each intrusion disguised as help.

Even her body conspired with her purpose. She had begun to wear Georgina's old silk shawls.

"Her ladyship said I might take what she no longer used" and though the claim could not be disproved, it settled uneasily in the mistress's throat for fear of accusation. The shawls looked *right* on her, which made them unforgivable. The imaginary whispers the same.

"It's as though she cannot remember her words, or her duty, or that she has a husband and children so who can blame Miss Marchwood for stepping into the breach."

Once, Georgina entered the drawing room to find Florence arranging primroses upon the mantel. Her sleeves were rolled neatly above her wrists; her dark hair shone against the pale blue of her gown. The sight was so gentle, so domestic, that Georgina felt, absurdly, as if she were intruding upon her own life.

"I was told these should be placed here," Florence said, not turning. "Mrs Dobbs said the southern air keeps them fresh."

"That is not your task," Georgina replied, the words weary even to her own ears.

"No, my lady." Florence inclined her head. "I only thought to spare Mrs. Dobbs the trouble."

She brushed her hands together, scattering invisible dust. The movement was delicate, dismissive. To rebuke her further would have seemed hysterical and futile. And Georgina Spencer was never hysterical. Futile, perhaps. So she said nothing. And in saying nothing, allowed another small annex to be built upon Florence's quiet empire.

The evidence of conquest accumulated in refinements too subtle to indict. Plumped cushions, relit lamps, books rearranged not alphabetically but by colour as if Florence intended to teach even the shelves obedience. Every improvement made criticism seem petty and every kindness rendered protest, vulgar.

Charles noticed only the comfort. "Miss Marchwood has a gift," he said over breakfast, smiling faintly into his cup. "The house feels *alive again*."

"Alive," Georgina echoed, folding her napkin. "Yes. It does. Like a creeping vine."

He missed her meaning entirely and continued to read his paper. Florence's beauty, never ostentatious, had begun to exert its own theology. It was not sensuality that held the servants, it was *certainty*. She moved like a prayer recited too often to doubt. They lowered their voices when she passed, not from fear but reverence. Even Mrs. Dobbs, who had once ruled the staff with a will of iron and vinegar, softened her tone in Florence's presence as one does in church. And if the household worshipped, Charles merely knelt.

Georgina saw it forming in his eyes, the soft gleam that

precedes surrender. He spoke of Miss Marchwood with gratitude at first, then with admiration, and finally with the distracted affection of a man who mistakes peace for love.

She tried to reason herself out of jealousy. What accusation could she voice without sounding mad? That the governess moved too quietly? That she *calmed* the children too well? That her presence changed the weather of a room? No, those were not accusations, they were symptoms. And women who name their symptoms too plainly are sent to rest.

One afternoon, Georgina entered the nursery unannounced. The room was lit with spring light, gentle as milk. Florence sat in the rocking chair, Hattie in her lap, the child's face tucked against the governess's heart. They were laughing softly over a doll dressed in miniature mourning clothes, black silk, plaited hair, eyes too bright.

"What do you call her, darling?" Florence asked.

"Mama Florence," Hattie said without hesitation. The next sound cracked the air.

"Hattie!" Georgina's voice struck like glass. "That is *Miss Marchwood!* You will not call her such a thing again!"

The child's mouth trembled. "But she loves me like a mama does," she whispered.

Florence rose, holding her close. "Please, my lady," she said, her tone low, unflappable. "She meant no harm. Children confuse affection with names."

Her voice was tender, almost pitying in an apology shaped like a caress. The humiliation, however, was complete. Georgina turned and left before her face betrayed her.

That night, while the house slept, Florence sat at her small desk beneath the dormer window. The candlelight made a golden chapel of her solitude. The snowmelt on the lawn below reflected the moon in broken pieces, like scripture scattered by wind.

She opened her journal.

He looks at me as a husband should. I see it in his eyes when I enter the room, the warmth that rises, the stillness that follows. He listens when I speak. He does not listen to her. The Lord rewards patience. The proud are brought low. The meek inherit the hearth.

She wrote in an even hand, the lines straight and devout, until something in her pulse grew swifter. The words began to lean, bolder now:

The child calls me Mama. The house breathes when I pass. Even the walls have learned my name. It belongs to us now, to him, to me, to the children. The old order has passed away. I have been faithful, and my reward is near.

Her pen faltered only once, at the final sentence. She dipped it again, deliberately, and wrote:

Florence Spencer.

The ink shone, black and lustrous as confession. She traced the name with her fingertip, smudging it just enough to make it *alive.* Then she closed the book, extinguished the candle, and sat a while in darkness. Below, the corridors murmured as they settled, wood against wood, brick against brick And Florence, feeling the steady pulse of her dominion beneath her feet, whispered a single word into the dark. *Home.*

It began, as all hauntings do, not with a scream but with the smallest rearrangements of the world, a mislaid trinket, a borrowed scent, a door left open that ought to have been closed. At first, it was the *brooch.* A trifling thing of gold filigree, a pearl at its heart, a wedding gift from Charles, sentimental, not rare. Georgina had not taken it out in years. But one morning, preparing for a walk, she opened her jewel case and found the indent where it should have been. The velvet held its ghost, but the jewel itself was gone.

She told herself what women are trained to tell themselves: that she had misplaced it. A clasp had come loose. A maid had borrowed it for cleaning. There was no malice in such vanishings, only carelessness. In her heart though, she knew the truth yet doubted, still. Until she saw it again.

The nursery fire burned low. Florence sat by it, mending a child's pinafore, her head bent, her lace collar catching the light and there, nestled at her throat, gleamed the brooch.

It was *hers.* The sight struck Georgina like a fist laid flat against the chest, stopping the breath but not the heart.

"That is a lovely piece," she said at last, her voice the colour of thin glass.

Florence looked up and smiled, calm as an angel painted in tempera. "Thank you, my lady. It was a gift, once."

"From whom?"

"From a kind soul," she said, turning back to her stitching. "One who saw something worth cherishing."

The needle rose and fell, bright as punctuation. Georgina watched the firelight flash against her own jewel, saw it glow briefly, obediently, at another woman's throat. "You wear it well," she murmured, and left the room before her voice could break.

Later that afternoon, in the corridor, she caught another theft. Not of substance this time, but of *air.* The faintest trace of her own perfume, violet and cedar, a scent mixed to her order by a London perfumer who remembered no other client by name, lingered as she walked. She followed it instinctively, like a hound following its own lost trail. The scent led her to the drawing room.

Florence stood at the mantel, arranging tulips. The fragrance hung about her like approval. Their eyes met in the mirror above the fire. For a moment, it was like looking into a version of herself with the edges corrected, the same perfume, the same stillness, the same command disguised as gentleness.

"Your perfume, my lady," Florence said lightly, catching her gaze in the glass. "Yes, it is. Mrs. Dobbs told me it had been left uncorked. I feared it might spoil so replaced the stopper but could not resist sampling it's delights. I do hope you don't mind. It was only a drop."

Georgina's reflection paled beside the governess's calm and the double meaning in her sly words but she didn't rise to the bait. "How thoughtful of you to rescue it and no, I do not mind." she said.

It was only a scent. Only a trinket. But such small things were the territory by which women like her mapped the world. *Now even that country was being annexed.*

One evening, returning early from a call on the vicar's wife, Georgina reached the landing and saw that the door to her bedchamber stood ajar. Candlelight flickered inside.

She pushed it open an inch and saw Florence. The governess stood motionless at the centre of the room, looking around her as one looks upon a home newly purchased. Her hands were empty, but her eyes held ownership. They travelled slowly over the velvet chair, the dressing table, the miniature of Charles on the mantel. When she saw Georgina's reflection in the mirror, she did not start.

"I brought some linens," she said gently and pointed to the pile on the bed. "I thought to save the maid a job as I was passing."

"That is most gracious," Georgina managed, "but I would prefer it if you didn't enter our private rooms."

"Of course, my lady."

Florence dipped her head and passed her, leaving behind a thread of borrowed perfume that clung like mockery. The door closed without sound.

Georgina slumped into the chair by her fire, staring into the grate until the flames blurred into red lace. There was no confusion left in her, only clarity, terrible and absolute. This was not admiration. Not gratitude. It was *trespass.* And trespass is only patient until it owns the land.

The next morning, Mrs. Dobbs appeared at the door of the morning room, twisting her apron in her hands. Her face was pale with something that looked like loyalty worn thin.

"Forgive me, my lady," she said, "but I think I ought to speak."

Georgina set down her cup. "Then speak."

"It's Miss Marchwood," the housekeeper whispered. "She's giving orders. To the maids. To the gardener. To the cook. Always polite, but she says it's by your command. 'Her ladyship prefers it so,' she tells them. Or 'Lady Spencer would have wished it done thus. She even blames me. And they believe her, my lady, because she speaks it as gospel."

Georgina's pulse did not quicken; it steadied. "In my name?"

Mrs. Dobbs nodded miserably.

"Thank you," Georgina said. "That will be all."

When the door closed, she sat perfectly still. Her calm was no longer virtue, it was armour. The time for suspicion had passed. What remained was proof, sharpened and gleaming. Later she went to Charles's study. He sat with a glass of port, its surface catching the light like a red eye. He looked tired, older than his years, worn smooth by comfort.

"Charles," she said quietly. "We must speak about the governess."

He sighed. "Not tonight, Georgina."

"She has overstepped her place."

He laughed softly, indulgently. "You've never liked her. Women rarely do like one another."

"She gives orders to the servants in *my* name. She wears my things. She..."

He lifted a hand, weary. "My dear, must everything be suspicion? Miss Marchwood is indispensable. The children adore her. The staff respect her. And I..."

He stopped, too late.

"You what?" Georgina asked, evenly.

"I trust her," he said. "She brings peace to this house, Georgina. You might try to learn from her example."

The words landed with surgical precision.

"I understand," she said. And she did, just not in the way he intended.

She left him staring into the fire, the glass of port forgotten. In the corridor, the air bit at her throat. She gripped the banister and stood there until her hands stopped trembling. The house around her sighed and settled, the floorboards murmuring as though remembering other nights, other women. Beatrice had stood here once, she thought. Beatrice had known. And Beatrice had died. *Alone. Dead.* The words marched through her mind with the slow, deliberate tread of fate approaching.

27

There are nights that begin in silence and end in judgment. This may be one of them. I know that Mrs Dobbs has judged me and betrayed me to Georgina and now I must find a way, as I have always done, to vanquish my foes and survive. God called my name and wants much of me, therefore I cannot disappoint him. I ponder on another night such as this, when my existence here at Branleigh was threatened and I found a way.

This one began with the smallest sound, a cry, thin and pitiful, like a thread pulled through the air. The child's voice.

The corridor was dark, the lamps already lowered. I had been standing at my window, watching the mist rise from the fields like smoke from a drowned fire, when I heard him. Theodore. My sweet boy. My borrowed soul.

I moved without thought, and my hand found the nursery door before my mind found caution. I turned the handle and entered. Inside, the fire had burned to embers, painting the walls with slow, red breath. The rocking chair moved gently, back and forth, though no hand touched it. The cradle stood empty.

And there, in the chair, I sat, the woman I had become in this house. The governess. The surrogate mother. Florence Marchwood.

My gown was open, one shoulder bare, the bodice folded down. The child whimpered against me, his tiny mouth searching, his fists closing on the fabric as though kneading bread. My body ached with a tenderness so fierce it bordered on pain.

The door creaked. A shadow crossed the firelight. Annie Larkin stood there, pale as a moonflower, her hands clasped at her breast. Her eyes widened not in curiosity, but in horror. For a moment she said nothing. Her lips parted, then closed again. The fire snapped in the grate as if to shield her from the sound.

"Miss Marchwood," she breathed at last. "What are you doing?"

I looked up at her, the rhythm of the rocking chair unbroken. The child nuzzled against me, whimpering softly. My heart was a drum in my chest. The moment had already chosen its path and all that remained was to follow it.

"I was just trying to soothe him until you arrived," I murmured.

Her face twisted into pity, disgust, fear, all tangled together. She took a step back. "You can't," she said. "You mustn't. It isn't right." Her hand went to her mouth, as if the words had escaped her control. "I'll have to tell her ladyship. She would never allow this."

"You'll tell her and I will explain you were being idle and nowhere to be found," I repeated softly, like an echo that meant something else entirely.

She nodded once, clutching her shawl. "That's not true so don't make lies up about me. I'm going to tell her in the morning no matter what you say," she said. "What you are doing isn't natural."

Then she turned and fled, her footsteps running down the corridor like a child escaping punishment. I heard her sobs as she reached the servants' stairs. The door closed. The house swallowed her whole.

The baby stirred in my arms. I held him tighter, whispering, "Hush, my darling. Sleep. Mama will make it right."

. . .

Once the baby was settled, I went to my room and collected something I suspected I'd soon need, an item I'd squirrelled away for emergencies, mine or that of another. Then I made my way downstairs to the kitchen where I found Annie alone at the long table used by the servants. I noticed immediately the way Annie's eyes avoided mine, the way her hands trembled as she dabbed her eyes. But I noticed. I always notice. The Lord sends warnings before He sends deliverance, and Annie's trembling was the sign I needed.

It was not anger I felt, only duty. Some souls are too fragile to bear their knowledge. Pity is not mercy if it leaves the weak in torment and I could not allow such a simple soul to live her life in such a way, so I offered to make her tea and then, we could talk. She nodded, but I sensed she still held her grudge but was unsure whether to stay or hear me out.

Beatrice's medicines always lay in her locked drawer, and I had the key and on the occasion I found her sleeping deeply, I liberated a small bottle that lay amongst others and slipped it into my apron pocket.

In the kitchen, once I'd poured the tea, a few drops of the chloral hydrate, clear, sweet, faithful, fell easily into Annie's cup.

She smiled faintly when I brought it to her. "Thank you, Miss Marchwood."

"Drink up," I said. "And I will explain and then we will be friends again, you and I."

She drank without hesitation. The effect was gentle, merciful. Her eyelids fluttered as I spoke of children, of the baby she had lost and how she must understand the desire to care for another even if it is not your own.

"Sometimes," she murmured, "I think I hear him crying still, my baby. At night, in the dark." Her head drooped. "Maybe the Lord forgave me, after all because he sent me here, to care for another sweet child."

"He forgives those who repent," I said. "But sometimes He asks us to walk with Him a little further first."

When her cup was empty, I took her arm. "Come, Annie. I think you need some air and I will tell you my truth as we walk. I will take comfort from sharing it with you."

"Your truth?" she echoed drowsily. "What do you mean?"

"That I was also sent a vision of mercy," I told her. "My tale will bring you peace."

She followed me as a sleepwalker follows a dream, her feet unsteady, her breath shallow. The corridor was empty, the lamps dimmed. Outside, the wind moved through the trees, carrying the faint scent of thawing earth. We passed the chapel; the rose beds sealed under their winter pall and came at last to the lake. The water lay still beneath a thin film of mist, its surface holding what little light the moon could spare. The reeds whispered at its edge, thin as secrets.

I guided her to the bank. She knelt, obediently, her fingers clutching the grass for balance.

"Sit and look at your reflection," I said, pointing to the mirror image of her face and the moon trembling in the black water. "Look, your face is that of an angel, I swear it.And your child, he is with the angels, too, so don't feel sad."

She nodded slowly, her head bowed. "I imagine him to be happy, in heaven," she whispered. "I pray it is so but still I miss him."

"Yes," I said. "I understand."

For a moment we were sisters, two women bowed before creation, each believing herself chosen.

Then I placed my hand upon her shoulder. The flesh beneath my fingers was warm, trembling. "Annie," I said softly, "you should go to him."

She turned, puzzled. "Go... how?"

And then I pushed. The sound was small, a gasp, the sharp catch of breath as the air met the cold. She slipped into the lake like a dropped shawl, the surface parting and closing again. I held her head under the icy water, pushing it deep. There was no struggle, not really. The drug had done its work well. Her arms rose once, twice, then stilled. The ripples widened, caught the moon, and vanished. I stood at the edge, watching as her hair spread beneath the surface like dark weed. Her face, upturned, emptied, looked peaceful. Not drowned but absolved. A baptism in reverse.

"The Lord takes the weak first," I whispered, repeating the words I would speak at her grave days later. "He knows they could not bear the waiting."

When it was done, I knelt and dipped my hands into the water, letting the cold bite the skin. It cleanses, if you believe it does. When I rose, my skirts clung heavy and dark around my legs. I did not look back. There is no wisdom in watching the world reclaim what never belonged to you. The path back to the house gleamed faintly in the moonlight. I walked slowly, humming to myself the tune that had become both lullaby and creed.

Sleep beneath the roses, child...

By the time I reached the servants' door, the house the candle still burned in the nursery window, small and faithful. Inside, the baby would be dreaming, safe, steady, chosen.

I touched the latch with wet fingers and felt the wood answer like flesh. I lifted my skirts and bunched them tights so they would not leave a trail of water on the flagstones to betray me, then I made my way to my room. After I had hung my skirts to dry by the fire, I slipped into bed and smiled, content, saved. The Lord had tested me and found me obedient.

Tonight, I am tested once more and again, I shall not fail him or the child, my soul son, who needs me now more than ever..

28

The day was unseasonably still. Not the calm of comfort, but the breathless kind that stands before a storm. Florence had taken Hattie into the gardens, the child's laughter drifting across the courtyard like the last echo of innocence. It was the first time in weeks the governess had been absent for more than a quarter-hour. Georgina had been waiting for exactly that gap. She had not slept. She had lain on her back in the dark, hearing again Mrs. Dobbs's tremulous admission, *She gives orders in your name, my lady*. and Charles's gentle contempt: *Miss Marchwood is indispensable. Indispensable.* The word tolled through her like a funeral bell.

She moved quickly, quietly. Her slippers whispered over polished boards, the pulse in her throat a second tread. The servants were at their tasks. No one stopped her as she climbed the narrow stair to the rooms beneath the eaves. At the landing she paused only long enough to recognise the small brass door plate: MISS MARCHWOOD.

Her hand closed on the latch. She drew a breath and entered.

It seemed smaller than she remembered or was it barer, an

austere cell made devout by order. The bed was made as if inspected by an army sergeant and a single chair sat square to the writing desk. The Bible lay open to the Psalms, a sprig of pressed lavender marking a verse about refuge. The air carried starch, candle wax, and beneath both her own perfume, stolen weeks ago and now faintly consecrating the space.

Georgina stood still and listened to the blood in her ears. Her composure, thin armour polished by long practice had begun to flake, shedding like old paint. The quiet dared her as she searched. Method prevailed. Drawers, underneath precisely folded linen, beneath the mattress, behind the small glass: all obedient, all exemplary, all false. Order can be a screen. She felt the irritation that accompanies admiration and redoubled her care. Then she saw the trunk.

Dark wood, burnished lock, initials cut shallow as if unwilling to boast: F. M. It had come on the first day, carried by a taciturn driver who had not met anyone's eye. Georgina knelt and let her fingers trace the letters. The key waited in the lock, she turned it and the mechanism sighed.

Inside there garments wrapped in tissue, a prayer book that smelt of damp, a lace handkerchief embroidered with *F*, a child's ivory rattle incongruous as a bone at a banquet. Georgina lifted each thing with a distaste she could not banish. At the bottom her fingertips met resistance. The panel moved. A false base. Her breath caught even though she knew many trunks and valises had them. She found the hidden catch by feel alone. A click. The panel lifted, revealing a shallow compartment lined in faded green silk. Within lay a small packet of papers tied with twine, the knot stained and stiff with age. She hesitated, dread has its ritual, then tugged the string. It gave.

The first thing she saw was a clipping, type blurred by fingers that had handled it too often:

. . .

TRAGEDY AT RAVENBROOKE ASYLUM. SEVERAL DEAD IN NIGHT FIRE. PATIENTS MISSING.

She scanned the column. *...shortly after midnight... overturned lamp... among those unaccounted for is Emily Leonard, formerly the daughter of the late Reverend Leonard of Aylesbury...* The words swam and sharpened, swam and sharpened. Emily Leonard.

A thought returned with the weight of a verdict: Beatrice's murmured winter warning but what was it? *Reminds me of ... something I read once.* Georgina had given it no purchase then. Now it set its hook. She turned the clipping. On the back, in a hand she knew too well, small, neat, fervent, someone had written: *Deliver me from bondage, O Lord.*

A psalm to some. To Georgina, a confession. Her knees went. She sat on the floor with the brittle paper held in both hands like a relic. The air thinned; the small mantel clock began to hammer time as if striking a door. Shadows lengthened toward her, courteous and intent. It was true. The woman who slept in this bed, who sang her children to sleep, who wore Georgina's scent and in turn caused her to push Charles's patience to the thread was not Florence Marchwood. She was someone else. This Emily, perhaps. Someone broken into a shape that looked like virtue. Someone dangerous.

Georgina rose carefully, as if the room itself would tilt. The scent of candle wax and stolen violet grew cloying. She crossed to the window. Below, Florence walked hand in hand with Hattie, the child's head tipped back, laughter visible even at a distance. The tenderness of the sight made it obscene, varnish over rot. Her heart gave a hard, deliberate thud. Proof. At last.

But proof is fragile. What would Charles see? A jealous wife with a tattered newspaper. He would sigh, invoke peace, invoke gratitude, invoke anything but the cost of being wrong. She could hear him already, that gentle dismissal that made a fool of grief.

Still the truth stood like frost on the lawn, undeniable because it burned when touched. She pressed the clipping to her breast. Resolve returned, not as fervour, but as arithmetic. This house had been reduced to shadows. Now she knew which shadow cast the rest. Florence. Whoever she was. She had deceived them all.

Georgina Spencer, alone if she must be, would not be deceived again. She left the room like a woman escaping a tomb. The corridor stretched ahead, long, pale, watchful. Every board felt complicit. The paper rasped against her palm; she realised she had crushed it along one crease and torn it slightly. In her chamber she turned the key, put her back to the door, and waited for her breath to remember itself. In, out. In, out. The sound of the bolt steadied her better than prayer.

She smoothed the clipping on the mantel as one might calm a frightened creature. *Ravenbrooke Asylum Fire... Emily Leonard among the missing patients.* The name stood up in the light like a spectre that had finally learned to keep its shape. Memory threaded itself at last. Tremors in empty rooms. The private hymns invented and repeated. The muddy footprints denied with perfect calm. The possessive tenderness masquerading as duty. The order that was, in truth, a claim. The lullaby that had spread like ivy through the house. The annexing of her precious children. It all aligned with dreadful economy.

The suitable governess had been a mask. Beneath it, Emily Leonard, escaped from an asylum and enthroned by gratitude. Madness polished until it shone like piety. No wonder she was so familiar with scripture. The room tilted. Georgina took the dressing table in both hands to anchor the world. The mirror returned a face she scarcely recognised: pale, hollow-eyed, hair loosened by the day's trespass. Fear stood naked there for the first time in her life.

Beatrice knew. The memory rose, the Dowager in her shawl, voice thin but certain. *She frightens me. I have seen that look in the chapel at the hospital... it's in the eyes.* Georgina had laughed, gently, indulgently. *You worry too much, Mama. Miss Marchwood is a godsend.* And Beatrice, shaking her head: *The Devil never knocks. He is in the house before you hear him.*

Prophecy, laid at her feet, stepped over. She sat, hands interlaced so tightly the fingers blanched. The paper breathed on the mantel. The house, alert as a hunting dog, seemed to incline its head and listen for her next move.

29

Downstairs, the grandfather clock struck four. Soon she would return. Florence. The saint of Branleigh Park. Georgina could see it all before it happened, the door opening, the cold shaken from her cloak, that practiced smile soft as candle wax. She would unbutton the child's gloves with tender precision, stoop to kiss her curls, murmur something about angels. Then she would lift her into her arms and ascend the stairs to the nursery where Theodore waited, his small hands reaching toward his mother-that-wasn't.

A nausea so violent rose through Georgina that she clutched the arm of the chair to steady herself. *My children.* Her children, placed nightly in the arms of a stranger and worse, a creature whose gentleness was mimicry, whose prayers were stolen from the lips of the dead. She crossed to the window. The air outside was thick with mist, rising from the ground like smoke from an invisible pyre. Between the yews two figures emerged, wavering first, then distinct. Florence in her dark cloak, Hattie beside her, the child's small hand lost in the glove that held it. Even from this distance Georgina could see the quiet choreography in the tilt of the governess's head, the careful adjustment of the bonnet, the faint flash of gold at her throat. Her brooch.

The sight hollowed her knees. It was an image that should have soothed: woman and child, hand in hand, returning from the garden at dusk. But to Georgina, it was a scene painted by madness itself, serenity turned inside out. How could she have been so weak to have not acted when she saw the brooch the first time. Was it her breeding that made her shy away from scenes and the shame of a spectacle that would shine a light on her own husband and his infatuation. She could not bear the thought of Florence, that woman, twisting the situation with lies, insisting it were own, cheap brooch given by her parents and not that which Georgina had carelessly lost. She could not bear the image of her husband taking that woman's side, and the servants hearing of it and sniggering below stairs. That was why she had kept her pathetic counsel.

She turned from the window, breath shallow. On the mantel lay the evidence, the brittle clipping. Proof, irrefutable and useless. What could she do? If she carried it to Charles, he would smile that tired husband's smile reserved for women whose reason had grown inconvenient. He would speak of rest, of nerves, of gratitude for the woman who had rescued his household. He would remind her who was the breadwinner, who toiled in London and kept the house afloat and deserved, expected, some respect for all he provided and some peace in his own home. He would defend Florence with the quiet conviction of the deceived.

Georgina pressed her palms to her temples. She must think clearly. She must not allow fear to sound like hysteria. Not for herself but for Hattie, for Theodore. The sky darkened by degrees. Frost turned to silver on the glass. A maid knocked, asking if her ladyship would dine. Georgina refused. The thought of food, of light, of conversation beneath that roof was intolerable.

Hours passed. The house settled into its nocturne. Then came the footsteps above. Light, measured, assured. Florence returning the children to their beds. Then came the sound, soft, rhythmic, infinitely patient. *Creak. Pause. Creak.* The rocking chair. The noise moved through the ceiling, through the plaster, into her brain and bones. She pressed her hands to her ears but the sound was already inside her, steady and alive, like another heart grafted to her own. *Creak. Pause. Creak.* Her mind painted the picture with dreadful clarity. Florence in the nursery, seated in the chair, Theodore curled against her breast, the fire gilding her face with its false warmth. The slow sway, the whisper of skirts, the slyness beneath breath.

Georgina bowed her head. The tears came quick, hot, noiseless, purged of grief. Not sorrow, but rage. The rage of a woman who sees evil seated in her house and is forbidden to name it.

At last she spoke aloud. "*Lord,*" she whispered, "*deliver us from evil, though it wear a gentle face.*"

The air, the house, God, seemed to listen. Above her, the chair moved once more, long, slow, final, and then the sound stopped. The silence that followed was worse. It was not peace. It was *waiting.*

30

The morning began with deceitful gentleness. Georgina had not slept. She had sat all night by the window, fully dressed, eyes fixed upon the paling dark. Thought had circled thought until exhaustion made clarity. *Enough.* Proof or no proof, she would speak. She would name the trespass aloud. The resolve steadied her hand but not her pulse.

By midmorning, Branleigh Park had resumed its ritual disguise with the clink of china from the breakfast room, the muted footfall of servants, the scratch of Charles's pen from his study. Georgina moved through the corridors with measured poise, her composure so perfect it might have been armour. She meant to confront him privately, to ask, to demand, to strip the lie bare. But as she neared the music room, a sound stilled her. Voices. Low. Close. Followed by laughter. Her hand froze on the door.

For a moment, cowardice begged her to turn away. Then she turned the handle. The room swam with morning light. Dust motes rose and fell, fragile as confession. The pianoforte stood open, the ivory keys catching the sun like teeth. And beside it, too near, far too near, stood Charles and Florence. He leaned against the instrument, one hand resting on its polished edge. His face wore that unguarded warmth she had once thought belonged only to her. Florence stood just within his reach, head tilted, eyes upturned, the faintest smile on her lips. Between them hung an intimacy invisible but undeniable, as if the very air acknowledged it.

The silence that met Georgina's entrance was total. Charles straightened, colour draining from his face. Florence drew back a pace, arranging her expression into remorse yet her eyes, dark and knowing, gleamed with something perilously like triumph.

"I beg your pardon," Georgina said, her voice calm and cutting. "I didn't realise the music room had become your *salon*."

Charles flinched. "Georgina, it isn't..."

"I think it is."

Florence lowered her head in graceful contrition. "Forgive me, my lady. The master asked me to fetch a score for Miss Hattie's lesson. I fear I lingered too long."

"Yes," said Georgina. "You did. You linger everywhere."

The words struck like frost. Florence's lashes flickered. For a heartbeat she almost smiled, then curtsied, perfection made flesh.

"You should go," Georgina said.

Florence hesitated just long enough to let the hesitation speak, as if waiting for Charles to intervene. Then she glided past, her skirt brushing Georgina's gown, a deliberate touch, intimate as a whisper. The scent of violet and cedar trailed after her.

When the door shut, the silence thickened. Charles remained by the piano, his hand still on its rim as if he required its balance. He would not look at her. For a moment, Georgina only watched him, this man, the father of her children who had once promised her the constancy of his soul and had since bartered it for calm. Then, before thought could intervene, her hand moved. The slap resounded like a gunshot. Charles staggered, eyes wide, cheek blooming red.

"You've brought shame beneath this roof," she said, the words trembling but precise.

He stared at her in disbelief and humiliation, something wounded that made him look absurdly young. "How *dare* you..."

"How dare *I*?" Her voice sharpened, rising at last through weeks of suffocation. "You've allowed that woman to take *everything* from me. My children, my home, your respect. I am a stranger here, Charles, a mere ghost haunting my own house."

He turned away, rubbing his temple, retreating behind reason. "You exaggerate. You've been overwrought since my mother's death. Florence, Miss Marchwood, has only tried to bring peace and give you respite."

"Peace," Georgina repeated, and laughed, a sound so brittle it cracked the air. "She's brought nothing but poison, and you've called it something else to suit your own vanity."

He faced her then, mouth set, eyes cold. "She has known sorrow, Georgina. You would do well to learn compassion."

"Compassion?" Her tone dropped to a whisper. "No. What you seek is *absolution*."

The words landed like steel.

He winced. "You speak as though I've sinned."

She met his gaze. "You have. You've handed her our lives and called it charity."

He muttered something she didn't catch, a prayer or a curse, and crossed the room.

"I won't be spoken to like this, not in my own home," he said, voice tight. "When you've regained your reason, we'll speak again."

"Reason," she echoed. "You mean obedience. Tell me, Charles, do you even know who she is?"

His hand froze on the latch. "She's a better woman than you've become."

Then he was gone. The door closed softly behind him, and the music room seemed to contract. The silence that followed was enormous. Georgina stood unmoving, trembling not from fear but from the knowledge that something within her had broken, cleanly, irreversibly. The piano's open lid threw her reflection back at her, pale, hollow-eyed, almost spectral. She pressed her palms to her face and drew a breath that burned. Outside, the sunlight shifted, cold and merciless. It fell in a thin bar across the carpet, illuminating the exact spot where Florence had stood.

Georgina looked at it for a long time, then whispered, "Not for much longer."

The battle for Branleigh Park had begun.

The house did not sleep so much as *wait*. It held its breath beneath the weight of midnight, listening to itself as if for confession. The rafters creaked softly, the walls exhaled in drafts and even the fire in the great hearth downstairs burned with a kind of nervous restraint. Branleigh Park, for all its stone and symmetry, had learned the language of dread.

Georgina moved through its arteries with a candle trembling in her hand. The flame bent and straightened with every breath she took. Her reflection flitted across the long windows, pale, insubstantial, her night-robe a thin veil between resolve and ruin. The carpet was kind enough to muffle her steps. The air smelt of lavender and faint smoke, Beatrice's candles. Florence burned them each night in the nursery, claiming they calmed the children.

Georgina had told herself she was going only to *look*. To see her children asleep, safe, untouched. But her pulse knew better.

No mother visits her children at midnight unless she fears she's already lost them. The nursery door stood ajar, letting a sliver of light spill into the corridor. She pushed gently. The hinges made a sound like a sigh.

Inside, the air was golden with firelight, soft and deceptive. Shadows moved like breath along the walls. Theodore slept in his cradle; fists closed tight as buds. Hattie lay in her little bed, curls damp against her cheek, mouth parted in a half-smile.

And by the hearth, in her rocking chair sat Florence Marchwood. The chair moved in slow rhythm, creak, pause, creak, each motion measured as if timed to the beat of her pulse. She was singing. That same lullaby that had begun to gnaw its way through the fabric of Georgina's nights.

Sleep beneath the roses, child,

Dream where angels weep.

The voice was gentle, tender even, but hollowed out, devotion without mercy. Florence looked up. The light struck her face, carving it into contrast, serenity above, something feverish beneath.

"They sleep best when I sing," she said softly.

The chair creaked on. Between them stretched the hush of a church before a sermon, Georgina set her candle down. Its flame leaned toward the governess as though it, too, recognised the gravity of what was about to be said.

"Your time here is done, Miss Marchwood," Georgina said, her voice stripped of tremor. "You will leave Branleigh Park tomorrow. I'll speak to Lord Spencer myself."

The rocking slowed. Florence's hand rested on the chair's arm, but the chair itself continued its motion, as if reluctant to stop. The lullaby died in her throat.

"You would send away their mother?" she asked, almost gently.

The words struck like a bruise. Georgina steadied her breath. "Their mother," she said, "is standing before you."

The statement landed between them like a blade. For three rocks of the chair Florence did not speak. Then she rose. Shadows followed her, obedient as servants. Her eyes gleamed dark and alive.

"You don't deserve them," she whispered. "You feed them tradition and expectancy, not love. You pray for them, but you don't *know or see* them."

"I see you," Georgina said. "And I will not let you near them again."

Florence's mouth curved into something that might once have been a smile but had grown sharp with conviction. "You think he will listen to you? He no longer looks for you in rooms you occupy. He looks for me. The children look for me. When they cry, it is my name that stills them."

Georgina stepped closer. Her shadow merged with Florence's on the floor, two shapes grappling before their bodies dared. "If you ever set foot in this room again, you will regret it."

The governess drew a long breath, as though tasting the challenge. Her gaze dropped briefly to the cradle, to the sleeping infant whose breath puffed against the blanket like the ghost of forgiveness.

When she looked back, her voice was calm again, even reverent. "As you wish, my lady."

She turned. Her hand brushed the baby's coverlet, a farewell, a claim, a promise. Theodore stirred and whimpered, then sank back into sleep.

"Leave," Georgina said, her tone final.

Florence lingered a moment longer, her eyes lifting, meeting Georgina's across the heat of the fire. "I shall," she murmured. "But only in body, never in spirit."

She passed by, unhurried. Her skirt whispered against

Georgina's gown once more, a touch lighter than breath, heavier than threat. The faint scent of violets followed her into the hall. When she was gone, silence returned like a held breath released.

The fire hissed and the children's soft breathing filled the room. Georgina moved to the cradle. Theodore's face was utterly serene. Hattie murmured and turned toward the wall.

"I will not let her take you," Georgina whispered. The words came out like a prayer and a curse in one.

She reached for the rocking chair. It still moved faintly, carrying on the ghost of the rhythm Florence had left behind. Georgina pressed her hand against it until it stopped. The final creak echoed, slow, reluctant, final. The nursery stilled. Yet Florence's presence clung to the walls like moisture after rain. Georgina turned toward the door, her candle's flame shrinking in the draft as she closed it and then she sat to keep vigil over her children.

The silence was complete. And in it, Georgina understood something colder than fear and a fact undeniable. Florence Marchwood had not left the room. Only her body had. The essence of her remained and waited.

31

Snow fell in fine, ceaseless veils, softening the angles of Branleigh Park until the house seemed carved from silence itself. The lawns were drowned beneath white and the trees stooped beneath their weight; the sky and ground met in a single pale oblivion. It might have looked peaceful to anyone passing through the gates, a portrait of winter calm, but inside, Georgina sat in the morning room, her spine straight, her hands folded over one another like paper.

The fire burned brightly, yet its heat reached nowhere near her. Before her on the escritoire lay a single sealed letter, the wax still soft and glistening. The address, the governess agency in Oxford, gleamed in tidy, deliberate ink. The pen beside it bore a trace of red wax, as if even it had bled a little in the writing.

She had not slept. Her night had been a vigil, a long rehearsal of resolve. The conclusion, when it came, had been simple and final: *it must end.* Whatever affliction possessed Miss Marchwood, whatever sin she cloaked in devotion, it could no longer be allowed beneath this roof.

When morning came she summoned the nursemaid and

gave her strict instructions to sit with the children, to not leave the room or their sight, and under no circumstances allow Miss Marchwood entry. Should she attempt to do so the nursemaid was to ring the bell and summon the butler. It was clear from her reaction that the nursemaid had never in her life been given such an order and the burden of it brought tears to her eyes, yet she nodded and obeyed, leaving Georgina so carry out that which had to be done.

There was a knock at the and when Mrs. Dobbs entered, her voice was careful, her eyes lowered. "Miss Marchwood waits in the hall, my lady."

"Send her in."

Florence appeared a moment later, composed as ever, though her complexion carried the faint transparency of sleeplessness. Her dark gown was buttoned to the throat, her lace cuffs folded with faultless precision. But her eyes, those too-bright eyes, held something fevered, as though an incandescent light had found a home there and refused to leave.

"My lady," she said, curtsying.

"Miss Marchwood," Georgina replied, her tone a blade. "Sit."

Florence obeyed. Her hands folded neatly in her lap. Only a tremor, slight but unmistakable, betrayed the strain.

"I have written to the agency," Georgina began, the formality of her diction keeping her anger in check. "I have informed them that your services are no longer required. I have not intimated why as I do not want the business of this house shared with others but that is the only reason I have not laid bare your behaviour. I wanted you gone today and requested Mrs Dobbs call for a carriage, however, the road is blocked but will be cleared by morning. You will leave Branleigh Park tomorrow."

Florence blinked, as if struck by something invisible. "My lady?"

"You will depart by noon. A carriage will take you to Oxford, where no doubt the agency will arrange your next post. In the meantime, you will be required to remain confined to one of the spare, servants rooms we reserve for those accompanying our visitors. You will collect your belongings and vacate your quarters immediately and stay away from the nursery and the children. Is that understood?"

The clock marked a single second, loud, surgical.

Then Florence said, very softly, "You cannot mean this. I hoped that last night was merely a fray of temper and by morning you would be calmed and realise this is all a mistake, a misunderstanding."

"No mistake," Georgina answered. "Your conduct has exceeded every boundary of service. It ends now."

Florence drew a deep, tremulous breath. "You don't understand," she murmured. "I have *devoted* myself to this house, to your children. To you. There is no one who loves them more."

"Love," Georgina said, her tone steady and glacial, "is not possession. You have mistaken your place."

Florence rose then, her eyes glinting, her restraint thinning to transparency. "It was *God* who brought me here," she said. "Do you think chance delivered me to your door? No. He chose me. He sent me to them. This house is my purpose."

"Do not blaspheme," Georgina snapped. "Whatever delusion you suffer, it ends today. Pack your things. You will not return."

For an instant, the governess seemed to sway, caught between collapse and explosion. Then her voice dropped to a whisper, thin and sharp. "You will regret this."

The words hung like smoke. Georgina's reply did not come. The silence was enough. Florence curtsied, shallow and stiff, then turned. The door closed with unnatural gentleness behind her.

Only then did Georgina's breath release, shaky and cold. Relief came, thin as air after almost drowning. It was done. She crossed to the window. Outside, the snow continued its quiet occupation, blurring the world into something that looked like purity. The sight brought her a fragile calm. By tomorrow, Florence Marchwood would be gone, dismissed, exiled, erased from the story of Branleigh Park. Perhaps then the walls would loosen their hold on grief, and the house would remember how to breathe.

Behind her, the fire cracked faintly. The letter gleamed on the desk like a promise fulfilled. She did not see the shadow that passed across the threshold, nor hear the light scrape of movement in the corridor. She did not feel the eyes fixed upon her from beyond the room eyes clear, cold, and bright with vengeance. She stood by the window, believing, for the first time in months, that she was safe.

Florence's footsteps echoed down the passage, calm, deliberate, like a procession no one dared interrupt. But when she reached her small chamber, the sound broke. The door slammed. The lamp flared, then stuttered, filling the narrow room with a wild, uneven light.

Everything was too neat. The bed, the folded linen, the Bible laid open to Psalms, all of it stared back at her with silent reproach. Obedience mocked her. Humility sneered.

Her breath came fast and thin. The words *you will not return* rang in her head, clanging like a bell struck from within. She crossed to the desk and tore open the drawer. The relics waited there, quiet as witnesses, her clippings, her proofs. *Beatrice Spencer: Dowager Lady of Branleigh, Dies Peacefully at Home.* The Ravenbrooke article, yellowed and brittle. A lock of child's hair wrapped in muslin. Trinkets that light fingers had collected and squirreled away. The fragments of a life she had pieced together from ruin. She gathered them all in trembling hands.

For a moment she only stared as if the paper itself might defend her. Then, slowly, something broke. The sound she made was neither sob nor laugh but something caught between. And then she began to tear. The first rip was clean. The next came harder. Soon the air was full of it, the sound of a life unmade. *Emily Leonard. Ravenbrooke Asylum. Unaccounted for.* The words lost meaning as the shreds fell. Blood welled from where the paper cut her palms, streaking the white pages with proof that she was still flesh.

The scraps drifted to the floor like snow.

"Emily," she whispered.

The name escaped her before she knew she'd said it.

And then came the voices.

Miss Leonard, please remain calm. The injections will help you rest.

You brought shame upon this house, girl. You will repent until the Lord hears you.

Her father. The doctor. The past.

She pressed her hands to her temples, shaking. "No," she whispered. "Not there. Not again."

But the memories crowded closer. The scent of ether. The crackle of burning. The door that never opened.

Her voice dropped to a hiss. "He sent me here. He chose this house. I am His hand."

The fire spat an ember that leapt onto the hearth, writhing for a moment before settling into glow. Florence's gaze followed it. The light flared in her pupils, two tiny suns.

Smoke had been her first language. Fire, her only absolution.

She crouched, pressing her wounded palms to the boards until they left faint red crescents in the grain. "They would cast me out," she murmured. "But I belong here. This house was chosen. I was chosen."

The flames rose, greedy and bright. She stood slowly, her eyes fixed upon them. The heat painted her cheeks with something like resurrection. Around her feet lay the ruins of every name she had worn, daughter, patient, governess. Only the purpose remained.

Her whisper was barely sound.

"If I cannot stay," she said, "then none of us will leave."

The wind outside moaned through the chimney, a low, trembling note. The fire answered, a hiss, a breath, a vow. And Branleigh Park, as if it heard, shivered in its bones.

32

Night fell hard upon Branleigh Park. Wind clawed the shutters and the trees thrashed like penitents in the dark. The moon went down behind a lid of cloud and the air sharpened, tasting of snow. Inside, the house lay taut and listening, praying for salvation.

After being confined to a dingy room for the whole day, her meals being brought on a tray and left at the door like a prisoner, Florence waited for dark and the house and its inhabitants to sleep. Now, she moved along the servants' passage like purpose made visible. The lantern in her hand threw brief, violent halos across the walls, light, dark, light, a stuttering heartbeat. In the other hand she carried a dented canister of lamp oil. Each tilt drew a thin, gleaming thread to the skirting, the oil beading and running, obedient as ink under a ruler. She traced the corridor, the back stair, the turn to the lower hall.

Her face was composed. It might have been prayer, not madness, guiding her hand.

At the stair's bend she paused. A draught loosened the strictness of her hair and lent her a girlishness that did not belong to her history. She lifted the lantern and met the painted gaze of Lady Beatrice Spencer. The gilt frame had dulled; varnish had softened; but the grey eyes remained keen, catching the small quake of flame.

"You understand, I know it," Florence whispered, tender as confession. "They mistook you for frail. But you saw me. You were kind."

The flame trembled. For a blink the portrait seemed ready to step down and approve. Florence bowed her head, obeisance, farewell, and went on. The oil followed, a thin black serpent coiling in her wake. Outside, the storm gathered its skirts. Branches scraped glass. Somewhere a shutter tore loose and banged like a late-arriving verdict. Florence did not start. She crossed the ground floor, slipped past the east wing where the nursery slept above the morning room below. The household had surrendered to bed; even the wind seemed to hold its breath as her hem whispered over boards.

She paused in the great hall and lifted the lantern toward the gallery of Spencer's, powdered, whiskered, ringed, stern. "It's only fair," she murmured. "We'll go together."

Then she turned and finished her drawing of lines.

In her room, Georgina sat at the escritoire, a tremor in the hand that held her pen. Each time the wind pressed the panes the lamp guttered and recovered, like a nerve learning not to flinch. On the paper, her writing marched in dark, urgent strokes. Next door, his annoyance and shame doused by brandy, the recipient of her letter lay in a stupor, no doubt hoping that by morning, noon to be precise, a new day would erase the memories of his infatuation and eradicate the gossip amongst the staff. His place as head of the household would be reinstated and the whole silly caper forgotten.

Charles, I can no longer endure the deception that has taken root in this house. You are blind to it, perhaps wilfully so, but I am not. I will not risk our children's safety nor my sanity any longer. Tomorrow I shall take Hattie and Theodore to my mother's in Surrey. You may join us, if you choose, when you remember what a husband's duty means.

The pen bled a bruise of ink. She set it down and listened. The storm's fury had gone muffled by stone; the house answered with its old, slow creaks. Far off, a door slammed, wind, she thought, or a careless bolt. She signed: *Georgina Spencer.* She blotted, folded, laid the letter aside. Calm arrived like a cloth over fever. *Done,* she thought. *The first step out.*

Then the smell reached her. Faint at first, an acrid thread through the hearth's honest smoke. The fire itself was low and contained. Yet the odour thickened, oily, determined. Curious, Georgina crossed the room. Near the door the air ran warm over her skin. She opened it. A thin veil of haze lay along the corridor ceiling, delicate as ribbon. Beneath it, unmistakable. Lamp oil.

Her pulse stumbled. *You will regret this,* Florence had said that morning, eyes bright as a blade. A gust rattled the windows. Georgina turned for the stair, the letter forgotten on the desk. From overhead came the first soft crackle of tinder discovering its vocation.

By the nursery, the corridor already hissed with burning oil. Fire moves quickly when given a line to follow. It licked the boards, tasting upward, casting a pulsing light like a monstrous heartbeat. Florence climbed the last steps. The lantern's flame shrank, rallied, steadied. Her face had taken on that pale luminosity certain saints wear in bad paintings. She reached the nursery door and listened. Inside, warmth; the sweetness of milk; the slow wash of sleeping breath. She slipped in and pressed the door to. Her fingers found the key. The bolt slid home with the quiet of a sentence being punctuated. The lazy nursemaid hadn't followed her ladyship's instructions and having left her postfor whatever reason, the punishment she should expect made Florence smile.

One lamp burned beside Hattie's bed. The grate held a quiet ash-glow, thin orange under pearl. Florence set her lantern on the table where its glass shivered with the tremor in her hands. She looked to the cradle. Theodore slept swaddled tight, the small rise and fall tidy as a metronome. On the pillow beside, Hattie's curls pooled like spilled gold.

Florence crossed and blew out the lamp. Darkness fell, relieved only by the grate's faint pulse and the lantern's small heart.

A voice, drowsy and trusting: "Miss Florence? Why is it dark?"

Florence knelt, smoothing a curl. "Hush now, dearest. We're going home."

"Home?" Hattie's brow furrowed. "But we are home."

"Not this one. A better, most perfect one. The one where no one cries."

She lifted Theodore. He made a soft complaint and settled, his head warm beneath her chin. She breathed him in, powder, milk, the impossible clean scent of life. Below, a door slammed. Voices rose, first uncertain, then shaped by fear. Smoke nosed under the nursery door in grey threads.

From the courtyard side, shouts, "Fire! The east wing's alight!"

Florence closed her eyes and swayed, clutching the child closer. His weight steadied the hand that had drawn the lines. Warmth answered warmth. *Not forsaken,* she told herself. *Not yet.*

"Miss Florence?" Hattie again, small hands gripping the coverlet. "What's happening?"

"Nothing to fear, my darling," Florence murmured. Her voice

slipped into the old cadence, the one that turned breath into spell. "The angels are coming to fetch us. We'll go together, you, and baby, and me."

Outside, boots pounded. Servants shouted through smoke. Heat bloomed through the floorboards as if the house had taken fever.

In the nursery, Florence settled into the rocking chair while smoke gathered low, stroking the floor, curious and hungry. It curled around the chair's legs, tasted the spindles, admired the polish. Theodore stirred. She began to hum.

Sleep beneath the roses, child,

Dream where angels weep...

The tune rode the crackle, thin and steady, absurdly pure.

"No one will take you from me," she whispered, tears carving pale tracks through soot. "Not now. Not ever."

The chair found its rhythm and kept it, creak answering roar, lullaby answering alarm. Heat pressed against the locked door. Flame flung itself at the panels like a body as Florence pressed her cheek to the child's hair. "Home," she said, as if the word itself were a key. "We'll go home."

She rocked once more, twice, the chair crying out like a hinge in an old church, smiled serenely and waited for salvation.

33

The first sound was the bell. It began faintly, an uncertain clanging, faltering and irregular, but it grew fast, gathering urgency as it rolled through the corridors of Branleigh Park like a metallic scream. Each toll struck the air with blind insistence, rattling the shutters and shaking the dust from the ancient beams. The house, accustomed to silence, seemed to cry out against itself. Then came the smoke.

It rose from the east wing in a black and oily cloud that coiled beneath doors and seeped along stairwells, thick with the stench of varnish, paint, and burning drapery. The fire had found its voice, low at first, then exultant, licking up the wallpaper in great curling tongues that ate their way to the ceiling. Curtains bloomed into flame as portraits warped and ran, faces that had stared down generations melted into colourless blurs.

The corridors filled with confusion. Barefoot maids stumbled from their quarters, coughing and sobbing into shawls. Footmen shouted orders over the din, voices cracking in the heat. From outside came the clash of buckets and the shouted rhythm of a chain line from the well. The courtyard churned with figures, stable boys, labourers from the estate, Charles at their centre, shouting through the smoke.

"From the well! Keep them moving! Don't stop!"

The wind tore through the broken windows and gave the fire breath. Flames leapt greedily from room to room, feeding on air, on polish, on memory. The house, which had stood a century, began to groan under its own undoing.

Through the chaos Georgina ran. Her nightdress was grey with soot, her bare feet slipped on the warped floorboards, her hair hung loose and wet against her face. The smoke bit her throat until she could barely breathe. She could see almost nothing, only the pulse of orange light ahead and the shapes that flitted through it like ghosts.

"Where are they?" she cried, her voice shredded by the heat. "Hattie! Theodore!"

A figure lurched from the haze, Mrs. Dobbs, her cap half torn away, her face slick with tears and ash. She clutched Georgina's arm, panting. "My lady, the nursery! I went up there immediately but... but she's taken them inside! The nursemaid went to use the privy and ..."

Georgina's heart stilled. "Who?"

"Miss Marchwood, and she's locked the door!"

For a second there was no time, no sound. Then Georgina tore herself free and ran, screaming for Dobbs to fetch the master.

The corridor to the nursery was a corridor of hell. The air shimmered with heat, the walls glowed red, blistering under the strain. Sparks fell from the ceiling like infernal snow. The smoke clawed at her eyes, at her lungs; every breath was a wound. Above her, the beams creaked, the groaning of a body preparing to die.

At the nursery door the handle glowed dull red. She hesitated only long enough to draw a breath, then seized it. The metal seared her palm instantly. She cried out but did not let go. Smoke poured from beneath the frame, thick and grey as velvet.

She threw her shoulder against the door. "Hattie!" she screamed. "Theo!" Her voice broke on the syllables. "Open, please God, make it open!"

No answer came but the roar of the fire and the faint, hollow thunder of boots in the corridor behind her. A stableman appeared through the haze, a bucket in his hand, his voice hoarse with terror. "My lady, get back! The roof's ready to come down!"

Georgina shook her head, her voice barely a whisper. "My children are in there!" Her fists hammered against the door again and again. "My babies!"

Charles came running through the smoke with his valet, Hardwick, close behind, an axe in his hands. His face was black with soot, eyes red and streaming. Georgina, half-blinded, still pressed her burned hand against the door, her strength draining with every breath.

"Stand back!" he shouted.

The axe fell once, wood splintered but held. Twice, shards flew, the impact echoing like thunder. Fire crawled up the walls, feeding on the silk wallpaper. Sparks leapt at their feet.

"Hurry!" Georgina cried, her voice breaking. "They're inside, hurry!"

A final swing. The lock gave with a crack. Charles kicked, and the door burst open, coughing out a great billow of smoke that rolled over them like surf. For a moment the corridor disappeared, the world reduced to flame and choking light. Georgina pushed past him before he could stop her.

The sight struck her like a fever vision. The nursery burned with a terrible, sacred beauty. The curtains were fire; the air shimmered like molten glass. In the centre of the room stood Florence, hair unbound, her dress scorched to grey ash at the hem. The baby squirmed in her arms, crying weakly. Her lips moved around a melody both soft and dreadful.

Sleep beneath the roses, child,

Dream where angels weep.

Her voice floated above the fire's roar, pure as glass, serene as madness.

"Florence!" Georgina gasped. "Give me the baby... please, we must go!"

The governess turned. Her eyes gleamed with something beyond reason, beyond grief. "He is mine," she said. "You cannot take him. He is mine."

The baby wailed. Georgina lunged, seizing the blanket, dragging it toward her as fire fell from the ceiling like sparks from a forge. Florence fought, clawing, her face transformed by fury and devotion.

"Lord, forgive you for he is mine," she sobbed, "Lord, forgive... "

Georgina tore the infant free and stumbled back. The child screamed in her arms, face wet with soot and tears.

Charles crashed through the smoke, scooping Hattie into his arms. "Now!" he shouted. "We must go... "

The fire leapt higher, ripping across the ceiling in veins of gold and red. Georgina turned for the door, Theodore pressed tight to her chest. Florence lunged, hair flying, hands outstretched.

"You can't take them!" she cried. "They're mine, mine! God gave them to me!"

A sharp crack split the air. The ceiling above the hearth sagged, then broke. A beam crashed between them in a storm of sparks. Heat rolled across the room, blistering the walls. Georgina staggered, shielding the baby.

"Charles!"

He reached her through the smoke, his arm locking around her waist. "Come!"

They stumbled into the corridor, the nursery collapsing behind them. The roar was deafening, a sound older than speech. Georgina turned once. Florence still stood on the far side of the beam, haloed in flame, arms raised as if in prayer. Her face was turned upward, eyes bright, mouth curved in a rapturous smile. The house groaned deep in its ribs. Then the ceiling fell. A bloom of fire filled the corridor, driving Georgina to her knees. She wrapped herself over the child, choking, her hair singeing in the heat.

Charles hauled her up, half-dragging her down the stairs as servants rushed with buckets and shouted prayers. The bell went on and on, its frantic clang the voice of the house itself. Behind them, the nursery burned like a single, furious star, consuming Florence Marchwood, or Emily Leonard, or whatever ghost had worn both names, until nothing remained but ash, smoke, and the faint, vanishing echo of her lullaby.

Sleep beneath the roses, child...

34

Dawn came without colour. The sky above Branleigh Park was a flat pewter dome, the sun veiled behind a haze of smoke that still rose from the blackened carcass of the east wing. The nursery windows, once bright with morning laughter, now gaped like hollow eyes. The roof had collapsed inward; stone blistered and timbers twisted, their shapes grotesque as melted bone. A slow, patient wind moved through the ruin, whispering through rafters that would never again hear a lullaby. It carried with it the stench of ash, scorched linen, and something faintly sweet, or maybe just the memory of milk gone sour in the heat.

The fire had died at last, not by human courage, but by exhaustion. It had taken what it wanted, then left silence as its offering. In the courtyard below, the servants moved like revenants. Their faces were grey, their hands blistered and bandaged, their voices reduced to whispers. Buckets lay overturned in the mud; their rims iced to glass. The world had shrunk to small gestures, a hand on a shoulder, a murmur of condolence that no one heard. Mrs. Dobbs stood near the stables, her apron stiff with soot, her eyes empty. The cook wept openly into a smoke-stained handkerchief. Somewhere a horse stamped and whinnied, still mad with the scent of ruin.

Inside, the house was quieter still. The children had been brought to the morning room, one of only a few untouched by flame. The curtains were open and the window eased a crack to allow in fresh air such was the stench of smoke and ravaged things. The fire burned low in the grate, its light small but stubborn. Hattie sat upon the sofa wrapped in a blanket, her little hands clutched the wool as though it could keep her from remembering. Theodore lay asleep in Georgina's lap, his breathing shallow, his small hand wrapped in gauze.

Georgina looked scarcely human. Her hair hung loose, the ends scorched to grey. Her hands were raw and trembling, swathed in linen that darkened where the ointment the doctor applied, seeped through. Her skin was drawn tight over cheekbones, her eyes ringed in soot. Each time the children shifted, she touched them gently, her fingers hovering, as though terrified they might dissolve.

The doctor from the village had worked silently, bandaging her hands. The smell of carbolic filled the room. "They will heal, my lady," he said at last. "You must keep them clean. You were fortunate."

Georgina's gaze drifted to the window. Through a slit in the curtain she saw smoke still rising from the ruin, thin threads twisting against the grey.

"Was it luck?" she asked softly.

The doctor paused. He could not tell whether she sought comfort or condemnation.

"Her body," she said after a moment. "Have they found it?"

He glanced toward Charles, who stood near the hearth, motionless. His eyes were fixed on the horizon beyond the window, the shape of a man trying to see past guilt itself. His teacup stood untouched, its contents long gone cold.

"Not yet," the doctor said gently. "The east wing was… entirely consumed. It will take days to sift through."

"Nothing at all?"

"Only fragments," he admitted. "A torn piece of cloth. A brooch, half melted, gold, I think."

Georgina nodded once, eyes still on the smoke. "Only that."

The silence pressed down like water. Hattie stirred and whimpered in her sleep. Georgina's bandaged hand moved, smoothing the child's hair.

Then Charles spoke, his voice dull, heavy with exhaustion. "She's gone, Georgina. The fire took her. Let it be over."

She lifted her eyes to him. He looked older now as though every trace of vanity had burned away, leaving a kind of naked sorrow. He had said little since the rescue. Even *safe now*, the words he had gasped when dragging her from the flames, had sounded like a question.

"Evil doesn't burn," she said quietly.

He frowned. "What are you saying?"

"I saw her face," she murmured. "She smiled in it, Charles. She *welcomed* the fire. That was not death. It was…" She searched for a word and found only dread. "Some kind of completion."

The doctor shifted uneasily. "My lady, grief…"

"This isn't grief," Georgina said, her voice steady as frost. "It's recognition of evil."

Charles turned away, raking a hand through his ash-streaked hair. "Dearest, you are in shock. Florence is gone. What's left of her is dust. Let that be an end."

But Georgina's silence was not agreement. Outside, the wind turned. A new gust stirred the soot into motion, sending a dark ribbon of smoke rising into the ashen sky. For a heartbeat and only that, she thought she saw it take shape as a figure of a woman, head bowed, arms outstretched in benediction. Then the smoke unravelled, and the image was gone.

The doctor finished his work and withdrew, murmuring a prayer neither of them heard. Hattie stirred again. Georgina gathered her close, whispering, "Sleep, my darling. Mama's here."

But her gaze returned to the window. Smoke still rose like incense. *She is not gone*, Georgina thought. *She is merely waiting.*

By the third morning, the smoke had thinned to a pale veil that clung to the ruins. The day broke with a thin light that gave no warmth. The staff were doing their best to clean and remove debris, injuries and scorched lungs permitting. Georgina had made sure the doctor and his nurse attended anyone in need and instructed those too ill to work were to rest. Her gratitude for their bravery on the night of the fire knew no bounds.

The newspapers arrived with the early post, folded, damp, and faintly scented with rain and ink. On the silver tray outside Georgina's door someone had placed a small vase of winter roses. The petals had already browned at the edges. She carried the papers into the sitting room, where the children still slept, and unfolded the first sheet. The headline struck like a hand.

TRAGEDY AT BRANLEIGH PARK: NOBLE SACRIFICE OF A DEVOTED GOVERNESS.

The column sprawled in reverent tones across two pages:

A melancholy calamity has befallen the family of Lord Charles Spencer of Branleigh Park. In the early hours of Tuesday, a fire broke out in the east wing, believed to have been caused by a faulty lantern.

Despite the heroic efforts of the household staff, the blaze spread rapidly. Through the bravery of the family's governess, Miss Florence Marchwood, the children were safely rescued at the cost of her own life. Those who knew Miss Marchwood describe her as gentle, devout, and deeply attached to her charges. Her devotion, it seems, endured even unto death.

The words blurred, not from tears but from fury. She read them aloud, her voice thin and sharp: "Gentle. Devout. Deeply attached."

Charles stood by the fire, his clothes, those that could be salvaged still smelling of smoke. His hands, cracked and raw, hung at his sides.

"Listen to this," she said, turning the page. "*The governess, whose selfless act will long be remembered in the parish, is thought to have perished while shielding the Spencer children from the smoke. Lord and Lady Spencer are said to be in deep mourning.*"

Her hand shook. "They call her a saint."

Charles turned, eyes shadowed. "It's what people need to believe," he said. "Let them."

"They should know the truth."

"And what would that buy us?" His tone hardened. "Would you have her branded mad? Would you have the children pitied, the servants questioned, your name whispered in drawing rooms? The world wants angels, Georgina. It would never accept that we housed a demon."

"The truth," she said, folding the paper with slow precision, "does not ask permission."

He took it from her and dropped it to the floor. "It's over," he said softly. "The fire is out."

Georgina's eyes found his, cold, steady. "No," she said. "It's *awake*, in here," Georgine tapped her heart.

The silence that followed seemed to hollow the room. Even the clock on the mantel dared not tick too loudly.

That night the wind rose again. It moved through the house like memory, sighing, insinuating. The surviving timbers creaked, their voices strange in the stillness. Georgina lay beside her sleeping children, staring at the dying fire. When her eyelids closed, she did not find peace but something deeper and older than fear.

She dreamed of the nursery before the fire and the soft lamplight, the smell of lavender and beeswax, the slow rhythmic creak of the rocking chair. Florence sat by the hearth, her hair loose, her dress the colour of ashes. She held Theodore, still and silent, his face pressed to her breast.

"Give him to me," Georgina whispered.

Florence did not move. The light shifted, and Georgina saw her face pale as paper, the eyes two polished stones.

"Please," she said again. "He's mine."

Florence turned her head, slowly, deliberately, and in that motion Georgina felt time shudder. The firelight caught her face. It was Georgina's own. The same eyes. The same mouth. The same faint burn along the cheek. They stared at each other, twin and reflection, while the room filled once more with fire. Georgina reached out, but her double only smiled.

Then the world dissolved into smoke. And through it, faint but distinct, came the lullaby.

Sleep beneath the roses, child...

35

It was several days after the fire when Charles finally spoke of it, not of the blaze itself, nor of the ruin of the east wing, but of *her*. Outside, a fine rain fell upon the remains of Branleigh Park, hissing faintly where it met still-warm stone. The courtyard stank of wet ash and scorched earth. The blackened timbers steamed in the pale daylight, each breath of wind stirring a faint sigh from the ruins, as though the house grieved for its own undoing. Inside, the surviving corridors were dim and airless, the draperies drawn to keep out the smell of smoke. The east wing was sealed, its doors nailed shut until the surveyors could declare what might yet be made safe. But no one spoke of rebuilding. Rebuilding implied belief in a future, and the house, and those who lived in it, were not yet convinced they possessed one.

Charles sat alone in the study. The same room where Florence Marchwood had once stood beside the pianoforte, smiling with false humility as he praised Hattie's progress. Now the walls were streaked with soot. One portrait had been removed for cleaning, leaving behind a ghostly pale square, a reminder of something once beautiful and irretrievable. The curtains hung heavy with the scent of smoke and brandy. A tumbler sat before him, untouched, its amber contents clouded by the dull light of the rain-streaked window.

He did not look up when Georgina entered. She closed the door quietly, the faint rustle of her skirts the only sound between them. Her hands, still bound in linen, were trembling slightly, not from pain but from the effort of composure. Her hair, once arranged with the precision of habit, now fell loosely about her shoulders. The lines of exhaustion around her mouth lent her a strange new gravity, as though she had aged years in days.

"You asked to see me," she said.

Charles nodded without meeting her gaze. "Yes. I owe you the truth."

The words came haltingly, as if dragged up through resistance. He drew a slow breath, his fingers tightening around one another as though afraid of what they might reveal.

"I won't insult you," he said, "by pretending she didn't matter."

Georgina said nothing. Her silence pressed him to continue.

"There was an... understanding between us," he said at last, the word faltering in his mouth. "Not in the way you might imagine. Nothing physical." His voice wavered. "At least, nothing that could be called that. But there was... a fondness. A kind of sympathy. An emotional *misunderstanding*, I suppose."

"Misunderstanding," she repeated. The word was neither question nor echo, only judgment.

He looked up at her then, and for the first time in days, the mask of restraint cracked. "I never meant harm, Georgina. I was deceived by her gentleness, her fragility. She seemed so helpless, so in need of protection. I thought..." He trailed off, his voice fraying. "I thought she admired me. And I wanted to be worthy of that."

"And were you?" Georgina asked softly.

Charles hesitated. The answer, when it came, was small. "No."

The silence that followed was long and airless. Outside, the rain beat softly against the windowpanes, rhythmic as breath. Georgina moved to the glass and stood looking out. The garden beyond was unrecognisable, a wasteland of blackened shrubs and churned mud. The fountain lay shattered; its basin filled with soot-stained rainwater.

At last, she spoke. Her tone was quiet, stripped of ornament. "She reflected what you wanted to see. That was her gift."

He frowned, uncertain. "Her gift?"

"And your sin," she said.

The words landed like a verdict. He bowed his head. The rain intensified, its sound filling the room like penance.

When he spoke again, his voice was barely audible. "What would you have me do?"

"Nothing," she said. "There's nothing left to be done. Your weakness and lack of judgement almost killed our children and for that, I can never forgive you. Whether you can forgive yourself is your business, not mine."

He nodded, slow and hollow, as though she had confirmed what he already feared, that repentance was no longer possible.

They remained like that for a long time, separated by the small width of the room and the immeasurable distance between guilt and forgiveness. The fire in the grate had burned down to coals, but neither moved to feed it. At last, Georgina turned.

"The builders will come next week," she said. "The surveyor insists the east wing must be secured before the rest of the house collapses."

Charles looked up briefly. "Then we'll go to London?"

"Yes," she replied. "London."

Neither spoke of returning.

When she left, he poured the brandy at last but still did not drink it. He sat until dusk blurred the outlines of the furniture and the rain became part of the silence. The smell of smoke lingered, threaded through every fabric, soaked into his hair, into his dreams.

That night, he slept in the half-ruined house. The air was close and damp, the ceiling above him still stained with soot. When the rain finally stopped, the silence that followed was thick and unnatural. Then, faintly at first barely more than a murmur, a sound rose through the stillness. It drifted along the corridor, threading through the cracks of the walls like water through stone.

A woman's voice. Soft. Lilting. Threaded with sorrow.

Sleep beneath the roses, child,

Dream where angels weep.

Charles stirred. His hand moved across the blanket as though reaching for something just beyond its edge. The fire on the hearth gave a sudden pop, scattering sparks that danced across the rug. The singing did not stop. It grew clearer, not loud, but close, as if whispered beside his ear. He turned over, muttering her name once, half in denial, half in longing, and the shadow of a smile, tender and terrible, seemed to pass across his sleeping face.

The fire flared again, briefly illuminating the room. For an instant, it threw a shape upon the far wall, the outline of a woman seated in a chair, her head bent, her hands folded in her lap. Then the flame sank, and the shape was gone. Only the smell of smoke remained. And still, beneath it all, the lullaby continued, soft, unbroken, and full of an unspoken promise.

36

I woke into heat as other women wake into pain. The floor bit my palms with splinters and cinders; every breath flayed my throat raw. Smoke lay along the boards like a living thing, low, ravenous, finding my mouth each time I tried to raise my head. Somewhere behind me timber screamed, a beam giving way, the sound torn from the bone of the house, and the ash trembled as though afraid. I crawled. My knees slid through soot turned to paste with my blood and tears; under it the oak still burned, bright at the seams like scripture branded into wood. I counted each movement as a penitent counts strokes, forward, forward, never back.

The Lord shall test me by flame, I murmured, the words thin and broken by the smoke. I could taste oil in the air, that sharp little sting that makes lamps faithful and houses faithless. He refines silver. He will refine me. The lesson had been taught long ago in a colder room by a colder man, my father, hands clasped behind his back, mouth shaping Scripture like iron nails. The furnace proveth the vessels of the potter. He had said it when the bruises flowered; he said it when the child was carried silent from my bed. I say it now as the fire takes my breath and gives it back altered.

A lullaby tried to rise and would not hold. The notes came wrong, warped, as if each had been singed at the edge. Sleep beneath the roses, child... but my throat crushed the word sleep to ash. Other words came instead: dust thou art. Not a lullaby. A verdict.

Behind me the nursery moaned, a low sorrow beneath the roar. I knew that room the way a body knows a wound. I had rocked there until the chair knew my measure; I had smoothed the child's hair until hair and hand were one. The chair was voiceless now. The cradle no longer creaked. Fire requires no mother. Yet even as the heat pressed my back, the old possessions tugged at me, the chair, the tune, the weight of the baby in my arms and with them the faces I had laid down like playing cards to win my place.

The real Florence first, in the hush of the inn, her breath warm under the pillow; the body becoming parcel, then problem, then the weight I knew how to carry. You are dust, I told her and meant mercy. Then Annie at the lake, gentle soul, rosary wound through wet fingers; the water took her as a font takes a christening, only backward, only blessed by night. Then Beatrice: kind hands, clear eyes, the last to look and see beneath the paint. I had kissed her brow. I had pressed the blessing down. In the corridor afterward the carpet had been so soft my feet forgot what I had done.

The faces jostled nearer. The doctor at Ravenbrooke, dictating my name into his ledger citing delusions of motherhood, his pen hissing the words like steam. Then my father's collar white as bone as he spoke of chastening; the women in grey shifts counting their breaths to stay sane; the lamp overturned; the first miracle of smoke. Fire had written my name once before. It wrote it now again, large as a psalm across the rafters.

I found where the floor failed into a ragged threshold. The air shimmered, hotter, meaner, and through it I saw a brighter dark: the hall, lifting like a mouth into the stair. The runner had gone, bitten to the warp. Portraits on the wall with their melted eyes. Beneath the crackle came another rhythm, regular as a clock. The bell, frantic, the house crying its own anguish.

He will not forsake me, I told myself. I took the burned edge of the threshold in both hands and pulled. Skin stuck. Pain cleared my mind for one sharp instant, enough to hear more than flame and the thud of boots, hoarse names shouted through the smoke, Hattie! Theo!And Georgina's voice stretched thin as wire. Names I had said, held, owned. Names I had tried to graft into my blood. I turned from them as Lot's wife had, but ash is not as kind as salt. It clung and followed.

The corridor leaned, gave, leaned again. I went on hands and knees into a world reduced to three lessons, heat rises, smoke kills, crawl low. The lamp oil's finger had run along the skirting boards where I had poured it, and now flame licked it clean, elegant as a cat. My hair fell loose; I felt the ends curl and shrivel, smelled myself. I laughed, one sharp bark that cracked the chest.

Then came a draught, sudden as a slap. Cold air knifed into the smoke and made it boil. Ahead, a square of paler dark shuddered, a window, not yet claimed. I crawled toward it, the sill a shore. The latch burned; I wrapped it in my skirt and lifted. The sash gave with a sticky sigh. The night rushed in, honest, immense, threaded with snow. The flakes fell black at the edges where they met the breath of the house.

The cold struck my lungs like truth. I gulped it until the world steadied. Beneath me the ledge wore a fur of ice; the garden below was speckled with embers, small red eyes staring upward. Far off, men moved like ants with buckets, their shouts torn to ribbons by the wind.

Behind me the fire drew a deeper breath, the long intake before speech. I turned toward the nursery I had made and unmade. For an instant the world sharpened with the scorched curve of the cradle and the rocking chair tipped forward in a bow. The shelf of picture books standing at attention. The wall where Hattie's height was marked in pencil lines no one would read again. All of it gathered into one impossible moment of grace. Then the room blossomed, white and gold and roaring. A burst of heat struck my back, turning breath to blade.

The glass beside me cracked like gunfire and fell inward in bright shards.

Go, something said, not a voice but a command made of air and consequence. I swung one leg out, then the other. The ledge was narrow, slick with ice. I edged sideways, palms raw against stone, until there was no more wall, only air. The drop yawned open like a mouth. I did not measure it. I had been measured enough. I bent my knees and leapt as if into water.

The fall was not long, but it was complete. For that slice of nothing, memory unspooled. The inn window, the pillow's soft denial. Annie's hair streaming beneath the lake. Beatrice's final breath like forgiveness refused. The asylum door opening to rain. The word free whispered to no one. I said it again now, though the wind stole the sound.

The ground rose like a hard white mattress. Snow took my weight and heat and kept it. The flowerbeds, those prim coerced things, offered their winter bones as a bed, and I made do. For a long while I was only breath turning to frost, eyes blinking soot to tears. Above me the east wing burned like the open side of a kiln, spitting fire at the snow that dared fall through, furious, unrepentant. The snow hissed in answer, a quiet baptism.

I pressed my cheek to the crusted earth and listened. The world, astonishingly, still had sound that was not fire: a horse protesting its halter, a branch cracking beneath ice, a bell tolling the same grief over and over. My hands burned and froze together; I did not lift them. Breath formed a little cloud that drifted, returned, drifted again. I watched it as though it belonged to someone else.

I spoke once, because silence can turn a soul to furniture. "I am here," I said to God, to the house, to the name buried under my tongue. I would take the first that answered. None did. But the snow consented to fall upon my face like the indifferent blessing of a tired priest. The hiss of flame grew thin. Dawn hovered behind the smoke, undecided. I lay in the flowerbeds, cradled by what only grows when cut back, and

I understood the lesson the fire had always meant to teach: that the world ends, and ends again, and yet refuses to be finished. I closed my eyes and let the last warmth leave my palms. When I opened them, the sky had lightened by a breath. The house still burned, but with a weary mouth. The angels had not come. Neither had the warders. I was alone, and not. I was ash, and not. I was dust that remembered shape. And the song that had failed me in the smoke returned at last, thin and almost kind, carried on the hush of snow.

Sleep beneath the roses, child... I let it lie beside me and did not answer.

37

By late spring the sea at Dover recovered its old, pitiless brightness. Sun struck the chalk until it dazzled; gulls hung and reeled, their cries stitched through the clatter of porters' barrows and the neat, impatient click of bootheels along Admiralty Pier. A railway packet lay alongside, steam shouldering from her black funnel, paddle-boxes lettered in gilt, decks humming with that purposeful confusion departures prefer to arrivals, trunks chalked with initials, wicker hampers fat with sandwiches and fear, hatboxes in shy little pairs like the heads of cautious birds. The fog-bell, idle in clear weather, let fall one lazy note to remind the day that caution is never abolished by sun.

Among the queue at the gangway stood an Englishwoman in a plain grey dress, bonnet and veil pulled low though the heat pressed against cloth and skin. The veil softened her outline, lending anonymity the dignity it required. She held a modest carpet-bag against her hip and when the gangway jolted she steadied herself with a practised touch and, for a breath only, a faint irregularity showed in her step. It was a recent injury and not theatrical, the sort of limp a child acquires on a farm track and keeps by habit into womanhood, or the sort earned by running too far in a skirt too heavy, pursued by heat, or leaping from a window in the dead of night.

Her papers, when the uniformed inspector asked, were in order. The railway men liked a name married to a ticket and a destination to report to the Board of Trade if the sea misbehaved. She offered a folded sheet. He uncreased it, read without curiosity, and put his pencil mark where pencil marks made people feel important.

"Mrs. Daisy Northcott," he said, forefinger locating the clerk's ink. "For Calais."

She inclined her head. He lifted his hand and she passed.

On deck the air smelt of salt and engine-grease, of wet rope and hot paint. A steward, immaculate in white apron and glazed expression, footed a crate toward the hatch with that particular courtesy seamen keep for inanimate objects. Forward, the bell rang twice; below, a valve sighed; the paddles ticked over and were still, as if reassuring themselves that running would soon be required. A curate in an exemplary hat argued gently, to no purpose, about where his portmanteau wished to be. Two young men in town clothes laughed too loudly to persuade anyone they were born to seas. A woman with a shawl pinned tight pressed a fretful infant to her breast and looked the way all mothers look within a mile of water, as if she had made a bargain with Providence and waited to see whether the other signer remembered the terms.

Mrs. Northcott took her place along the lee rail beneath the shelter of the deckhouse. When the pier-lines were let go and the gangway run in, the packet drifted outward on the tide until the paddles bit and white water flared from the wheels like torn linen. The cliffs stepped back at once; the town flattened to a string of roofs; the castle crouched above it like a faithful dog. Spray blew off the bow and set a fine glitter upon the crape.

A few minutes only into the passage the infant decided to petition the universe: first the small exploratory cry by which babies enquire whether tears improve matters, then, receiving no amendment, a full-throated protest. The mother tried all the economies handed down the generations, a shift of hold, a soft pat, a promise of landfall and milk. The sea offered nothing and the ship rolled just enough to teach land-bodies humility.

Mrs. Northcott turned her head. The veil made her kindness indistinct, which is the kind most easily believed. She moved nearer without pressing, and when the mother, exhausted and embarrassed, lifted the wordless plea women are trained to swallow, the veiled figure inclined her head and began to hum.

Only a thread at first, almost private, a tune found, not performed. It nested beneath paddle-thresh and gull-cry and it sat under the wind and would not be blown out. The infant's furious face settled by degrees; the fists unclenched; the cry dwindled to those small, noble sniffs by which babies forgive the world for existing.

"Thank you," the mother said, colour peering through pallor. "He won't have it from me when the water moves."

"I used to sing that to my own," the veiled woman answered. The words were soft enough to be mistaken for innocence. No one else heard. The sea is discreet.

The crossing behaved by Channel standards, though a bank of haze lay to the east like a promise broken late. Gentlemen who had come ready with cigars were coaxed saloon-ward by a steward loyal to Admiralty by-laws while ladies settled against the benches' cushioned backs and watched one another's hats with the affectionate distrust of a small nation. Newly mandated cork life-belts, proud of their novelty, hung in a row like lumpy saints. Tea arrived, black and strong and not improved by milk that had spent an hour disliking the heat.

Below, the private cabin offered a strip of practical comforts that became luxury by being one's own. An oil-lamp swung lightly on its gimbal. The washstand kept a jug and bowl with a chip no one had thought to turn to the wall. A canvas strap crossed the lower berth to hold its occupant where society preferred her. Mrs. Northcott set her carpet-bag on the seat, drew the bolt with a care that did not quite amount to fear, and removed her gloves.

The skin beneath was pale where it ought to be soft, tight where softness had been taken. Along the heel of the right hand a seam of newer flesh shone like wet paper. She flexed the fingers slowly, laid the gloves aside, and unfastened the small trunk that had drawn no notice above because it was designed not to.

Linen folded to a discipline, rolled stockings, a phial of salts, the decent lie of a widow's equipment; and beneath, wrapped in a child's petticoat yellowing at the seams, one thing only. She lifted it as if it might speak. A baby's bonnet, not Theodore's but in her mind, she imagined it to be so. This one was stolen from a perambulator as she passed an unobservant nanny too engrossed in a shop window.

She set it on the coverlet and sat very still. Above, the packet altered course a point and the light shifted from grey to a paler grey. Somewhere a steward knocked to ask whether the lady would take broth. She did not answer. She listened to the small, exact sounds ships make when obeying orders, like the thrum, the sigh, the courteous complaint.

Presently she wrapped the bonnet again, slower, and returned it to its place. She closed the trunk, turned the key, and tucked it down into the seam of her bodice the way women tuck the last true thing they own. Standing, she opened the door a fraction and let the salt air wash the room. The veil she left in place. Widows are permitted to keep their faces.

On deck the haze thickened enough to make Calais a

smudge, then thinned to reveal the low French shore, the lighthouse set like a pin on pale cloth, the jetty with its seam of men in blue blouses. The tricolour lifted and fell, loyal to itself. A douanier shaded his eyes and appraised the packet with the sober vanity of officials. The bell rang and lines snaked outward; the paddles slowed, churning the harbour to broken plates of light.

Mrs. Daisy Northcott stood among the crowd and composed the posture of a woman arriving. The limp showed when she took her first step to the foreign pier; the gloves covered the lines the fire had written. Behind the crape her mouth shaped a tune no one heard because the harbour was noisy with welcome and commerce.

Sleep beneath the roses, child, the thought went but not the sound. *Dream where angels weep.*

Beyond the Customs shed a woman laughed, a child coughed, a porter swore at a crate that refused to weigh what he wanted it to. The world, having gone to ash, resumed its business. She adjusted the strap of her bag, offered her papers when asked, and was waved through with the other harmless Englishwomen whose names matched their tickets. France received her as ports receive the newly named, by not caring who they had been.

The weeks that followed were painted in light. Spring warmed without haste and even the ocean learned to breathe slower. By May the air in Biarritz had turned soft and salted, laced with orange blossom from the groves climbing the hills. The season's English colony, retired colonels, careful consumptives, and the idle rich, descended upon the resort like migratory birds in lace. Villas along the Grande Plage were newly whitewashed; parasols bobbed; the sea glittered like hammered silver.

Daisy Northcott rented two rooms in a villa whose stucco

had been persuaded into the shape of virtue. From the balcony she watched the morning build itself, fishermen shouldering nets dark with last night's salt. Basque women gossiping in a braid of languages that hid kindness inside complaint; a thin priest walking his rosary along the promenade as if it were a small dog he could keep from straying. She learned the cafe where the coffee was drinkable, the bakery where the crust spoke first, the stationer who wrapped paper as if words were perishables.

She learned other things. How to be spoken to as a person who had lost enough to be left alone. How to answer questions with weather. How to fold her hands so the scar did not announce itself, and how to let it show when pity might purchase silence. In the afternoons she walked the cliff path where wind kept secrets busy and water corrected cliffs, and she counted the ways a coastline offers departure without promising arrival.

Sometimes English voices caught at her ear, soft as moths, eager as debts. "Mrs. Elsworth, you *must* take the waters," or "My poor nerves, George; the journey quite undid me." She kept her head turned just enough to be unrecognised by strangers who had never known her. If a child cried, because a ribbon had escaped, because sand does not obey, she paused at a courteous distance and hummed two notes, then three. Often that was sufficient to distract and entertain. Mothers thanked her with the eyes women use when language would be too heavy to carry back to their tables. She never said, *I used to sing that to my own.* A person determined to live among the living must ration confession.

Letters could have found her had they been sent. None were. She posted two under her new name: one to a London agency whose ledgers recorded governesses like ships, one to a Mr. Vincent in Paris who arranged situations discreetly for ladies whose husbands had died inconveniently abroad. In both she wrote the neat hand of women who are believed. In both she said she was free to travel.

At vespers on a Sunday she sat in the cool nave of Sainte-Eugénie beneath a window full of orderly saints. The candles did what candles always do, dressed grief in gold and made it presentable. The priest's Latin moved like a tide across a reef. When the bell for the elevation sounded she bowed her head with an obedience that was not quite worship and could not honestly be called defiance. *Create in me a clean heart,* she said, as one might request a room with a view. The Lord, as before, declined to sign the register but did not eject her.

Summer came on in increments and shutters taught themselves to be useful; the sea took off its iron and put on silk. On a day without wind she went to the post and found a blunt envelope with Paris upon it. The letter within was civil as a man who knows the price of discretion.

Madam Northcott,

A family in the département de la Gironde seeks an English instructress for one child of tender years, with duties light and recompense adequate. Catholic sympathy preferred but not required. References to be furnished, passage remitted upon acceptance. If you are amenable, present yourself to the undersigned at the Rue de l'Abbé-Grégoire on Thursday next. Yours,

A. Vincent.

She folded the paper twice, then a third time, until it became no larger than a matchbox and exactly as dangerous. On the balcony that evening she watched the sea swallow coins of light and considered the map that had existed, all along, behind her eyes: the inn; the lake; the house; the pier; the foreign shore; the next door opening like a mouth that means to speak and has not yet decided upon words.

She opened the trunk, unwrapped the bonnet, and laid it on the bed as women lay relics before travel. The lace broke a little further along its edge. She did not mend it and remembered the day Theodore tugged and tore it with his chubby fingers.

At dawn she packed with the economy of those who have learned to carry only what will pass a stranger's hand. The veil she kept. The limp she could not help. In the mirror she arranged her face to the expression clerks prefer, of modest means, reasonable hopes, misfortune borne. The world, which had ended, went on. And Daisy Northcott, who had once been a woman with another name and another house and a fire that refused to finish what she started, who had wandered frozen and in pain until she came upon a small cottage on the outskirts of a village she did not know.

Inside, she spied a woman in widow's weeds, sobbing by the fire. A few more hours perishing in the snow were rewarded and when the woman hurried into the garden to fetch logs, the watcher slipped inside and hid in the pantry. The cold slab of the floor was infinitely warmer than the snow and after she covered herself with sacking, she slept at last. When night fell, and the distant church bell tolled three, the hour when humans sleep deeply, she slid from her hiding place and did what she did best and freed the widow from her misery.

Once it was done and morning came, she found items that laid the widow's life bare. A letter for her landlord explaining why she was leaving, in the hope of starting a new life where the memory of her dearest husband didn't torment her daily. Envelopes were lined up on the table, one with the final rent money, another marked 'savings' and the final one contained male items, a fob watch, a wedding and cygnet ring, cufflinks and army medals.

That night, by the light of the moon, she deposited the widow into the well, the sound of her body hitting the watery depth taking longer than expected. She remained at the cottage for only two days, allowing her body to begin the healing process and the pain in her leg to ease. Then, at first light she finished packing the case that lay on the floor and dressed in the widows Sunday best, gloves covering the ravages of flames, and walked towards the town in the distance, never looking back, only forward.

The envelopes containing money served her well, as did the trinkets which she pawned in London before heading on to Dover and then France. And now, she was about to embark on another leg of her journey, perhaps not the final destination but the Lord would guide her. Smiling at her reflection in the hotel mirror, Daisy took up her bag, opened the door and after a hearty inhale and exhale, pushed back her shoulders and went to meet the little ones who needed her next.

38

Among the servants who arrived with the season's influx was a new governess in the employ of a Mr. and Mrs. Temple, a young English couple "wintering abroad for the sake of the baby's health." She had come to them through the usual, respectable channels: a Paris agency of unimpeachable tone and vague origins, the kind that never burdened clients with the tedium of birthplace, references, or verification. The letter of recommendation was written in an elegant hand, the sort of penmanship that implies moral character.

Her name, entered neatly into Mrs. Temple's household ledger between *Cook, Maid* and *Nurse*, was Mrs, Daisy Northcott, Governess.

She was, by every visible measure, an excellent servant. Diligent. Soft-spoken. Tireless. She rose early and with purpose, her shoes polished to dull modesty, her hair concealed beneath a plain grey bonnet. She never lingered in the servants' hall longer than duty required, never gossiped with the French maids about their sweethearts or with the English nurses who gathered on the promenade to exchange ailments and recipes. She answered softly when addressed, smiled enough to seem kind but never eager, and her employers, particularly Mrs. Temple, whose heart was as malleable as her taste, agreed she was *exactly the sort of quiet Englishwoman one needs abroad.*

Each afternoon, as the tide turned, Miss Northcott could be seen pushing the Temples' infant along the promenade. The pram, a fine wicker construction with polished brass wheels, gleamed like a reliquary in the light. Her movements were precise, her posture immaculate. She neither hurried nor idled, keeping always to the paved edge where sea and sky made a seamless pale horizon. Other nurses chatted beneath the striped awnings, their laughter carried bright and brittle on the wind, but Miss Northcott stood a little apart, watching the horizon as if it were something that might one day bring her bad news or a visitor.

The sea was never still in Biarritz. It hissed and murmured over the black rocks, its spray ghosting the air with salt. The wind came off the Bay of Biscay smelling of brine and tugged at her veil, lifted the edges of her skirt, brought a false bloom to her cheek. Her eyes, however, did not change. They remained the colour of faded glass. When the infant stirred, she bent and began to hum. It was the same melody she had chosen always, the tune that had once hushed the nursery at Branleigh Park, that had endured the fire and the crossing, the same low, steady rhythm that made grief sound almost like comfort.

Sleep beneath the roses, child,
Dream where angels weep...

The sound carried, threading through the rush of the sea and the creak of wicker wheels. It drifted over the heads of promenading couples, slid through the salt air, and was lost where the tide curled upon itself. The baby, soothed by that ancient music, quieted at once. The tiny hands unclenched and the mouth softened into peace. Daisy smiled faintly although not from joy, but recognition. Her gloved hands rested lightly on the pram handle. The wheels turned again, slow and steady, keeping time with the sea.

A small boy, chasing a hoop along the path, stopped short as she passed. His nurse called sharply, but he did not move. He stared up at the veiled woman, transfixed, at the smoothness of her stride, the stillness of her shoulders, the way the veil fluttered but her eyes did not. The sunlight caught those eyes for a moment which were clear, colourless, the pale stillness of deep water before a storm.

He tugged his nurse's skirt. "That lady's eyes," he whispered. "They look like glass."

The nurse hushed him, flustered, pulling him away, but the child looked back once more before the promenade turned out of sight. The image remained of the silent English governess standing beside the sea, her veil fluttering, the pram white and gleaming beside her, the wind carrying a tune that sounded half lullaby, half curse.

Out beyond the breakers, a ship moved slowly and solemn toward the horizon, its funnel trailing a faint ribbon of smoke that thinned into the light. Daisy watched it until it became a smudge, then nothing. Her lips still shaped the melody, silent now, as if the sea had claimed the sound for itself. She turned and began the long walk back toward the villas, the pram wheels whispering over the promenade stones. Her pace was even, her gaze forward, unhurried, serene, as though time itself had consented to follow at her heel.

The gulls wheeled above, crying over the surf, white wings flashing against the sun. She did not look up. Her head moved occasionally and sought thc ocean again, eyes, pale and unblinking, were fixed upon the line where the sea met the light a horizon empty as grace, endless as her guilt. And somewhere beneath the rhythm of the tide, just low enough to be mistaken for wind, the lullaby continued.

EPILOGUE

Night came softly to Biarritz, folding the town in silk and shadow. The sea breathed against the shore, carrying the scent of salt, damp stone, and the essence of memory. From her narrow attic room above the Temple family's villa, the governess could see the line of the moon across the bay, a trembling blade of silver cutting through the dark.

Inside, order reigned. A narrow bed turned down with military precision. A porcelain jug cracked but clean. A single candle wavering in its dish. Against one wall stood a cradle, small, white, and from it came the soft, steady rhythm of a child's breathing, delicate, unbroken, like the sea murmuring to itself.

At the dressing table, Daisy Northcott brushed her hair. Each stroke was slow, deliberate, ceremonial, a kind of prayer disguised as routine. The mirror before her was cracked from corner to corner, dividing her reflection into jagged mosaics: one eye bright, the other dim; one half of her mouth tender, the other fixed and empty. The fractured woman in the glass moved in perfect calm.

She set down the brush and reached for a small diary. Its pages were worn thin at the edges, the paper smelling faintly of smoke. She opened it to a clean leaf and began to write. Her hand was steady, the loops of her script fine and meticulous, the handwriting of someone who has spent years mastering appearances.

The fire cleansed me. I am reborn. He lives through me, and I through him. We are together, always.

She paused, the nib trembling a fraction above the page. Her lips curved in a faint, secret smile. Outside, the surf whispered against the rocks like a slow exhalation, like something immense breathing in its sleep.

God has chosen me to keep him safe and sound, she wrote on. *To guide him through the darkness men call the world. I am not afraid. I am delivered.*

The candle sputtered, sending up a thin thread of smoke. She laid the pen aside and began to hum, softly at first, a low murmur that seemed to rise from her throat without conscious will. The melody was familiar, impossibly old. It had survived fire and salt and distance.

Sleep beneath the roses, child,
Dream where angels weep...

The sound floated through the dimness, filling the small room with its strange, tender melancholy, a hymn, a curse, a mother's promise remade as devotion. In the cradle, the infant stirred, a small whimper fluttering from its lips before sleep reclaimed it. Daisy tilted her head, listening, her pale face illuminated by the candle's last breath of light.

A gust rose from the sea, sharp enough to rattle the shutters. The candle flame bent and died. Darkness folded over the room, leaving only the moonlight, thin and cold, to silver the boards.

Then came the knock.

"Mrs. Northcott?"

She turned; her profile caught in the moon's edge. "Yes, madam?"

Mrs. Temple stood in the doorway, her shawl drawn loosely around her shoulders. Her face held that blurred gentleness of women long deprived of sleep. "Is the baby settled?"

The governess smiled, a mild, unhurried smile, perfect in its composition.

"He is, madam," she said softly. "Peaceful as can be."

Mrs. Temple exhaled, relieved. "You're an angel, Mrs. Northcott. I truly don't know what we'd do without you. Thank you for bringing him to your room. I feel like I haven't slept in an age. I will see you both in the morning."

The door closed. Footsteps receded. Miss Northcott turned back toward the cradle. The moonlight fell across it in a white bar, bright upon the infant's cheek. She moved closer, hands folded, the hem of her dress whispering against the floor.

"There now," she murmured. "Mama's here."

The child sighed and shifted. She reached down, fingers tracing the curve of its face, light, reverent, possessive. Then she began to rock the cradle. The motion was precise, hypnotic, the rhythm of tide and heartbeat. Her lips moved again, and the lullaby slipped into the air, soft as breath:

Sleep beneath the roses, child,

Dream where angels weep...

The cradle's hinges creaked in time with the waves outside. The melody wove itself through the sound of the sea, its gentleness gathering weight, its beauty sharpening into something close to menace. The child's breathing deepened, steadied, surrendered. Daisy's voice fell to a whisper, her words fading into the hush until they were no longer sound at all, only movement.

Outside, the sea murmured against the shore, the same low rhythm as the cradle's sway, the same slow pulse as the woman's hand moving back and forth, back and forth. And though the room was still, though the night was soft and silent, the hand that rocked the cradle never truly stilled.

Printed in Dunstable, United Kingdom

79376664R00131